# Anthony St. John

# PRIVATE SESSION

Book design by Anthony St. John
Cover design by Anthony St. John



ISBN: 979-8-9954637-0-2

Follow Anthony on his social media outlets from:

https://linktr.ee/anthonystjohn

I would like to thank God, first and foremost for his continuously guidance and love through this journey we call life!

To my family and friends: Thank for endless support making me to be the person I am today. Through the good, the bad and the ugly moments, you all impacted my life to make me a better person!

To the reader of this book: Thank you for taking the time to purchase and reading my book. I appreciate each and every one of you!

**Stay tune for other titles…**

# CHAPTER I

## New Genesis

Leaving is never a clean break. It is a slow, jagged peeling of skin from bone, especially after investing two decades of your life into a hollow shell of a relationship. For Nia Jefferson, Memphis has become a beautiful cage, and today is the day she finally picks the lock.

Nia and Mr. Kevin Sanders were the blueprint for "meant to be." High school sweethearts, the golden couple on the prom throne, voted most likely to build a dynasty. They followed the rules—mostly. Nia stayed local for community college, anchored by family loyalty. Kevin headed to the University of Tennessee to study accounting. That's where the rot started. The long distance was a graveyard of broken promises; Nia would wait by the window for a homecoming only to receive a last-minute text while Kevin was busy "studying" the nightlife and other women.

Still, Nia was a builder. She saw the grit and grace of her parents' marriage and wanted to mirror it. She earned her degree in Media and Journalism, landing a freelance writer position at the Memphis paper. Kevin returned with his degree and a job as a bank advisor, but his collegiate antics followed him home like a stray dog.

Nia is the kind of woman who stops traffic in Memphis. At 5’4”, with a thick, 175-pound frame and a complexion like warm caramel, she is the "catch" everyone talks about. She has that rare, street-smart wit—one minute she’s the poised church girl in the front pew, and the next she’s rolling a blunt and dissecting last night’s overtime game with the best of them. Kevin saw the way single men looked at her and the way married men regretted their choices. Fueled by a toxic mix of jealousy and possession, he coerced her into moving in thirteen years ago.

Thirteen years of mental paper cuts and blatant betrayals. Nia looks at herself in the mirror—"cute in the face and thick in the waist"—and wonders how she let a man dog her out so thoroughly. But the destination is set. The ghosting of Kevin Sanders is about to begin.

**7:10 AM.** The old wooden stairs groan under Kevin’s weight as he careens down into the kitchen. He leans over and brushes Nia’s cheek with lips that feel dry and crusty, like old parchment. He has no idea this is a series of lasts. Last kiss. Last breakfast. Last look.

Nia has already tucked her life into a red leather suitcase, hidden deep in the foyer closet. She moves mechanically, plating scramble eggs, crispy bacon, and buttered toast. The kettle lets out a piercing, high-pitched whistle. She pulls it from the flame, the steam clouding her face as she pours coffee into Kevin's favorite mug.

She sets the plate down on the floral place mat. Kevin doesn't look up. He reaches for the morning paper, snapping it opens to the sports section. There is no "Thank you," no "Good morning, baby." Just a heavy huff of air when she moves toward the sink.

*I won't miss that huffing shit when I'm gone,* Nia thinks, her back to him as she grips the edge of the counter.

She watches him struggle with his tie. Kevin is a mediocre advisor at best; he slides by on the labor of his secretary—his latest "side project." Nia sighs, walks over, and loops the silk around her own neck to execute a perfect military knot before sliding it back over his head.

"What about me?" she mutters under her breath, tightening the silk. "I'm horny from sunup to sundown and you're out gambling and spending checks on hotel rooms with dirty bitches."

For a second, she imagines tightening the tie until the life leaves his eyes, but she isn't looking for a prison cell in Mason. She forces a plastic smile, giving him one last window to be a human being. Kevin checks his watch and shoves a piece of bacon into his mouth.

"I'll be home around seven," Kevin commands, gathering his paper. "Have my dinner ready, bitch."

He walks out. Nia follows him to the screen door, watching his Ebony Twilight Metallic Buick pull out of the driveway. She listens to the squeak of his brakes at the corner until the sound vanishes. She returns to the sink, the hot water scalding her hands as she scrubs the grease from his plate.

Her mind wanders to the bitterness in his eyes. He blames her for the loss of their only child. Not a day goes by that she doesn't feel that phantom weight in her shoulders. The first trimester had been a minefield; the doctor warned them it was high-risk, but Nia had pinned her hopes on God. It wasn't in the cards. Maybe God knew what kind of man Kevin was.

But Kevin's favorite weapon is the reminder: *"How can you live with yourself, killing our child?"*

Nia wipes a salt-water tear from her cheek with the back of her hand. She unties her apron, drapes it over the chair, and picks up the house phone.

"I need a cab to 345 Willster Avenue. Now."

Thirty-minutes later, a soft knock sounds against the mesh of the screen door. Nia smooths her dress, takes one final, agonizing look at the house—the happy memories now strangled by the bad ones—and opens the door. A young man in his twenties stands there, tip-toeing the line of professional and Southern. He tips a black hat, his loafers polished.

"Nia…Ms. Nia Jefferson?? My name is Rick and I'll will be your driver for today. Do you have any luggage to carry to the car?" His voice is deep, like Mississippi mud.

Nia points to the red suitcase follow by a "Thank You". As he hauls the luggage to the cab, she pulls her house keys from her pocket, setting them on the table by the window. She locks the door from the outside, the click of the deadbolt sounding like a gunshot.

"To the train station, Rick," Nia says, sinking into the green cushioned seats of the yellow-checker cab.

"Train station it is, ma'am."

The cab hums with a low, rhythmic vibration as Rick navigates the morning traffic. Inside, the air is thick—not just with the scent of pine air freshener, but with the heavy, unspoken weight of Nia's departure.

Nia leans her forehead against the cool glass of the window. Outside, the familiar rows of suburban houses blur into a smear of brick and green. As the cab pulls away, she stares at the flower beds she spent years tending—vibrant marigolds and hydrangeas that now look like a life she no longer owns.

She fumbles with her phone, her thumbs hovering over the screen. She reminds herself to call her parents; she can't just vanish. The thought of Janet waiting for her in Detroit is a small anchor, but it isn't enough to stop the fear, which sits like a cold lump of ice in her throat. At every red light, the silence in the car becomes deafening. She wants to scream for Rick to turn around, to tell him this is a mistake.

Then, the memory hits her—the word *bitch* hanging in the morning air like smog back at the house. The sting of it keeps her mouth shut. Rick glances at her through the rearview mirror, his expression softening. He clears his throat, his voice low and steady.

"So, I gotta ask... where is a beautiful soul like yourself heading this early in the morning? You look like you're carrying the weight of the whole world in those suitcases."

Nia's heart hammers against her ribs—a frantic, trapped bird. She presses her palm against the cool leather of the seat.

"Detroit. I'm going to Detroit. My friend Janet... she's waiting for me."

"Detroit, huh? Motor City. I been there a couple of times. Had the best corn beef sandwich of my life from a place name Mr. Fofo's!"

Nia swallows hard, the lump in her throat feeling like jagged glass. She tries to keep her voice from trembling, but it cracks on the exhale.

"I have to go. If I stay here... I'm just waiting for the next word to be thrown at me. Like a punch I know is coming but can't block. I can’t breathe in that house anymore, Rick. The air is just... gone."

Rick nods slowly, his large hands steady on the steering wheel as he navigates a jagged pothole with practiced ease. He shifts his weight, turning slightly in the driver's seat to catch a glimpse of Nia in the backseat. In the dim, filtered light of the cabin, he studies the way she curls into herself, her knuckles white as she grips her purse. He’s seen that look before—the frantic scanning of the rearview mirror and the shallow, bird-like breaths. He can tell she isn't just heading toward a destination; she is running from something… or someone.

"I get it. Believe me, I do. Sometimes the only way to find yourself is to get off the map for a while. New scenery has a way of washing off the old dust."

"I just feel like I'm running away." She looks at her reflection in the side window, barely recognizing the woman staring back. "Does that make me a coward? To just leave while the house is quiet?"

Rick’s eyes meet hers firmly in the mirror, holding her gaze with a sudden, sharp intensity.

"No," he says, his voice dropping an octave. "It makes you a survivor. There's a big difference between quitting and escaping, Ms. Nia. One is giving up; the other is choosing to live."

They pull up to the station, a grey, industrial building that feels far too permanent for Nia's liking. Rick goes above and beyond, hopping out to set her luggage on a small-wheeled carrier. The station is a cacophony of sound: the hiss of steam, the distant metallic screech of tracks, and the hurried footsteps of commuters. Nia fumbles through her pockets, her hands shaking as she pulls out some lint, a sticky gum wrapper, and a few crumpled bills.

"Here," she whispers, her voice breaking. "For the help."

Rick sees the tears welling in her eyes, threatening to spill over. He doesn't take the money. Instead, he gently folds her hand back over the bills, his touch warm and grounding.

"Keep it. You're going to need a coffee when you hit the city. Just promise me you'll keep looking forward, okay?"

Nia nods, a single tear finally escaping. "Thank you, Rick. For everything."

"Please have a safe ride. God is with you!" Rick says softly

He waves and disappears into the Memphis traffic. Nia stands alone. She buys a one-way ticket to Detroit—a bridge to a life where she isn't a "bitch" or a "child-killer." She stops at the station store, buying chips, a soda, and a prepaid phone. She misses the 80s; she wishes there was a wooden payphone booth she could hide in.

She finds a bench in the departure area, her heart hammering against her ribs. She keeps looking over her shoulder, half-expecting Kevin to storm through the doors and drag her back to his cage. With shaky hands, she activates the sixty-minute phone card. She dials the only number that ever felt like home.

"Hello?" Ms. Ruby's voice is sweet, elderly, and cautious.

“Ms. Ruby... it's me. Nia."

"Oh, child! I thought you were a bill collector. How you, baby?"

"I'm okay, Ms. Ruby. How's Daddy?"

"Can't complain. Your father is out back messing with that old hunk of junk car again. I think he loves that engine more than me!"

Nia forces a small laugh. "He loves you, Ms. Ruby. He just wants to take his favorite lady for a spin." She takes a jagged breath. "Ms. Ruby... I'm going away for a while. I don't know when I'm coming back."

The silence on the other end is heavy, but it isn't the silence of confusion. It's the silence of a woman who has been waiting for this call.

"I don't blame you one bit, honey," Ms. Ruby says, her voice steady. "I thought this call would come sooner, but you held your own as long as you could. Where are you going?"

"Detroit. Janet is there. Ms. Ruby... I'm so scared." Nia lets out a sob, her head dropping to her chest.

"Oh, baby, you'll be alright. God is with you through the thick and the thin. Don't you worry about us. We can handle Kevin."

**"TRAIN 635 TO DETROIT IS NOW BOARDING."**

"Ms. Ruby, that's me. I have to go. I love you."

"I love you too, baby. Be safe."

The screen flashes *Disconnected.* Nia wipes her face, tucks the phone away, and hands her ticket to the conductor. She finds her seat, sliding past a stranger to reach the window. As the train jerks and begins to roll, she watches the Memphis skyline begin to shrink. On the platform, people are waving and blowing kisses to loved ones. For Nia, there are no waves. No blown kisses. Just the steady rhythm of the tracks and the hope that by the time she reaches the North, she'll remember who she was before Kevin Sanders tried to erase her again. It has been a long morning, and it is going to be a much longer night.

# CHAPTER II

## Love Doesn't Live Here Anymore!

Kevin pulls into the gravel driveway, the crunch of the tires sounding unusually loud in the heavy, humid evening. He kills the engine and stares at the house. It sits like a dark tomb among the row of modest Memphis homes. No flickering blue glow of the television in the window, no porch light to welcome him home.

He steps out of the Buick, his eyes narrowing as he scans the neighborhood. "Ms. Lawson's lights are on... Mr. Wilson's, too," he mutters, pointing a thick finger at the glowing windows next door. It isn't a power outage.

He tramps up the porch steps, the wood groaning under his weight. He yanks at the screen door and inspects the frame, looking for the splintered wood of a break-in. Nothing. He jams his key into the deadbolt, twists it with a sharp *clack*, and throws the door open.

Kevin fumbles for the switch, flooding the living room with the harsh, yellow glare of the ceiling fan light. The house is eerily still. The air feels stale, untouched. He tosses his briefcase onto the sofa and moves to the side table, where his eyes land on the ceramic dish. Nia's keys are there—nestled right in the center. He picks them up, the metal cold in his palm, checking the familiar keychain to be sure.

"Nia?"

Silence. He strides into the kitchen. The linoleum is clean, the counters bare. The stove is cold, the pilot light the only thing burning.

"NIA!" Kevin's voice erupts, a jagged tear through the quiet. "WHERE THE HELL IS MY SUPPER?"

He yanks his tie from his neck, tossing it onto the counter. The white fabric of his shirt collar bears a faint, greasy smudge of red—Chanel No. 9 lipstick that doesn't belong to his wife. Hunger claws at his stomach, fueling a rapid, bubbling rage. He storms toward the stairs, his heavy footsteps thudding like a heartbeat.

"If you're up here with someone, I'll kill both of you!" he rants, slamming his fist against the drywall as he rounds the banister.

He bursts into the bedroom. The bed is unmade, the sheets tangled and cold. This isn't right. Nia is meticulous; the bed is always tight enough to bounce a quarter off when I get home. He checks the bathroom, then the guest room. Empty. He jogs back downstairs, tearing through the kitchen to the back door. He flips the floodlights on, sending a pair of raccoons scurrying into the brush, but the yard is a ghost town.

He slams the door and sinks into a chair at the breakfast table. The faint, floral scent of another woman's perfume still clings to his skin, and as he licks his lips, he can still taste the salt of an after-hours betrayal. He stares at the wall for a long minute before pulling out his phone. He wipes his face, forcing his voice into a mask of calm, and dials Nia's parents.

"Evening, Ms. Ruby. Sorry to bother you so late, but is Nia over there?"

"Hello, Kevin," Ms. Ruby's voice crackles, sounding light and unbothered. "I haven't heard from her since yesterday. Is everything alright?"

"I'm sure it is," Kevin says, though his jaw is tight. "Just got home from a long shift. House is dark, no dinner. Just wondered where she got off to."

"She's probably just out for a stroll or stuck in the rush at the market," Ruby says. There's a faint edge of suppressed joy in her tone that Kevin is too self-absorbed to catch. "Go find something in the freezer, boy. Don't be so helpless."

"Right. Goodnight, Ms. Ruby."

He hangs up, staring at the phone as if it had lied to him.

Across town, Ruby Jefferson sets her phone down on the end table and walks back into the flickering light of the television. Her husband, Charlie, is perched in his recliner, a forkful of corn halfway to his mouth.

"Who was that, Ruby?"

"That fool Kevin, looking for Nia," she says with a sharp, satisfied grin. She sits down and takes a bite of her meatloaf, dabbing her mouth with a napkin. "That boy is about to realize he's played his last hand."

She checks the gold watch on her wrist. "It's a long ride to Detroit. I'm hoping to hear from our baby by morning. You want me to wake you when she calls?"

Charlie tilts his glasses down to the bridge of his nose, his eyes shining. "Does a pig squeal when you pull its tail? You wake me up the second my baby girl's voice hits that line. Now, hush up—Matlock's about to get to the good part."

The train let out a long, metallic hiss as it ground to a halt in Gary, Indiana. The station was a desolate stretch of concrete and yellowed fluorescent lights, the only stop on the long haul north.

"Thirty-minute layover," the conductor announced.

Nia stepped off the car, her joints stiff and her mind racing. The night air was crisp, smelling of diesel and lake water. She wandered over to a row of battered vending machines, her throat parched. She fed her last few coins into the slot and pressed the button for a water.

Nothing.

She pressed it again, harder this time. The machine hummed mockingly, keeping her money and her water.

"Good morning, young lady. May I?"

Nia jumped slightly, turning to see an older gentleman. He wore a sharp tan suit under a black trench coat; a black derby hat perched perfectly on his head. He looked like he'd stepped out of a different decade.

Nia stepped aside, curious. The man glanced left, then right, ensuring the platform was clear. Then, with a speed that belied his age, he delivered a thunderous kick to the base of the machine. *CLANG.*

A bottle of water and a can of orange soda tumbled into the tray. Nia reached down, laughing in spite of herself. "Thank you, Mr...?"

"Albert Jenkins. And who might you be, pretty lady?"

"Nia Jefferson. It's a pleasure, Mr. Jenkins."

They found a nearby bench as the wind whistled through the station. Albert pulled out a pack of Newport, offering her a loosie. She shook her head. He lit up, the blue smoke curling into the rafters.

"So, what's a girl like you doing on a midnight train to nowhere?" he asked, his voice a pleasant rasp.

"Minding my own business, thank you very much," Nia shot back with a wink.

Albert let out a booming laugh that turned into a cough. He wiped a tear from his eye. "You got spice, kid. You need that. Too many people out here think they're God's gift, but the second they hear 'no,' their ego bruises like a rotten peach."

Nia sighed, the weight of the weekend pressing down on her again. "Honestly, Mr. Jenkins? I'm going to Detroit. To see a friend... and to start over."

"Detroit! HELLO, DETROIT, I love that song." Albert said, his eyes lighting up. "People think we're just rust and ruins, but if you want a city that lets you move at your own pace, that's the one. You'll do just fine there."

He paused, glancing at her bare ring finger and the shadows under her eyes. "So, where's your man? A girl like you shouldn't be traveling this far alone."

Nia looked down at her lap, her breath hitching. The memory of Kevin's face—the sneer, the lipstick on his collar, the years of "bitch"—hit her like a physical blow. Albert reached into his pocket and handed her a crisp, white handkerchief.

"Keep it," he said gently as she wiped her eyes. "I'm sorry I hit a nerve. I'm sure you have your reasons, and no one has a right to judge 'em. But I've got a remedy for that tension. It's the secret to a long life and a clear head."

Nia looked at him, waiting for some profound piece of wisdom. "What is it?"

"Fucking," Albert said plainly.

Nia's jaw dropped. She felt a surge of indignation, ready to slap the old man, but he held up a hand.

"Hear me out, kid. My wife and I? Fifty years. Five kids, three grandkids. We've had fights that would level a house, but they always ended with us resolving it in the bedroom. Communication is the lock, but sex is the key that tells you if the door is really closed. I'm not saying go be a hoe—unless you want to, then by all means, 'Just Do It' like the shoes say. But don't let your body stay as tense as your mind. A good release is a holy thing."

Nia stared at him. It was crass, it was blunt, but it was the most honest thing anyone had said to her in years. Kevin had used sex as a weapon or a chore. She'd forgotten it could be a release.

“Mr. Jenkins... I think I needed to hear that.”

“My pleasure, Nia. This old body won’t be around much longer, so I might as well pass on the truth while I can.”

The conductor’s whistle blew. “All aboard! Ten minutes!”

Albert stood up, offering his hand to help her up. He leaned over and kissed the back of her hand with old-world gallantry. He pressed a small business card into her palm. “If you’re ever on Conner Street, stop by my TV repair shop. I’ll fix your set for free.”

“I will, Albert. Thank you.”

Nia boarded the train, her mind buzzing. She sat down, pulling a thin blue blanket over her knees. She looked at the card—*Jenkins TV Repair*—and then glanced at the sleeping man in the seat next to her. Albert was right. She was a ball of knots and fury, and she needed to let it go.

She waited until the train began its rhythmic chug-chug out of the station. She excused herself, stepping over the sleeping passenger, and made her way to the tiny bathroom at the end of the car.

The door locked with a click. She leaned against the sliding door, the vibrations of the tracks humming through her heels. She closed her eyes. She didn't want to think about Kevin. Instead, she thought about Derrick Cooperfield, the star of her favorite soap opera "Sunlight through the Tunnel". His deep voice, his chocolate skin, the way his muscles had rippled under his suit as he held Gloria in his arms when he rescues her from Todd.

Her breath grew heavy in the cramped, dimly lit space. She let her dress slide up, her fingers finding the heat she'd ignored for far too long. The train lurched, a sharp turn on the tracks sending a jolt through her body that she incorporated into her own rhythm. She bit her lip, stifling a moan as the tension of the last thirteen years began to center and coil.

Faster. She focused on the phantom touch of a man who was kind, a man who was strong. She felt the climax rising like a wave, higher than any mountain in Tennessee. When it finally broke, it wasn't just pleasure—it was an exorcism.

Nia leaned over the small stainless-steel sink, her forehead against the mirror, gasping for air. The frustration, the anger, and the scent of Kevin's house seemed to wash away in the drenching heat of the moment.

She cleaned herself up, straightened her dress, and stepped back out into the aisle. She felt lighter. The shadows under her eyes didn't feel quite so heavy. As she settled back into her seat and watched the Indiana cornfields blur into the darkness, she felt a strange, new sense of peace.

Detroit was coming. And Nia Jefferson was finally ready to meet it.

# CHAPTER III

## Motor City, Here I Come!

It is 3:00 AM in Memphis, and the night is thick with the sounds of the deep South. Outside Nia's parents' window, the crickets are in a frantic, rhythmic party. Near the curb, a pair of raccoons are mid-heist, clattering the unlidded metal trash cans as they scavenge for a pre-dawn feast.

Inside, the sudden, shrill chirp of the cordless phone pierces the silence. Charlie jolts awake, his hand fumbling blindly across the nightstand, knocking his glasses to the floor with a soft *thud.* He presses the receiver to his ear, his head still heavy against the plush pillow.

"H… Hello?" his voice is a gravelly, sleep-crusted growl.

"I can't find her! I've looked everywhere, and I can't find her stupid ass!" Kevin's voice is hysterical, vibrating with a mixture of panic and wounded pride.

Charlie cracks one eye open, squinting at the glowing red digits of the alarm clock. "Who the hell is this?"

"It's Kevin!"

"Boy, it is three o'clock in the damn morning," Charlie snaps, his patience evaporating instantly.

Beside him, Ms. Ruby is already alert. She reaches over, her eyes knowing and sharp, and pries the phone from her husband's hand. She motions for him to go back to sleep. She stays silent, listening to Kevin rant about Nia being missing, her face a mask of calm.

She stands, cinching her robe tight as she walks down the hallway toward Nia's old bedroom, wanting to give Charlie some peace. She sits on the edge of her daughter's childhood bed, the floral comforter cool beneath her.

"Kevin, the writing is on the wall," Ms. Ruby says, her voice steady and cold. "She *left* you, son."

The line goes dead silent. The words hang in the air; a truth Kevin has been sprinting away from all night.

"No… I don't believe that, Ms. Ruby!" Kevin's volume spikes, his desperation turning into aggression. "I just saw her this morning! Everything was fine! She helped me with my tie, for God's sake. I told her I'd be back for supper. You know where she is. Tell me where she is! I need to talk to her!"

"Now, you wait one damn minute," Ruby interrupts, her voice dropping an octave. "Don't you dare raise your voice at me because *you* made the bed that you're currently losing your mind in. I don't know where my baby is, but I know she's in God's hands. And that means she's safe from you."

She rubs her forehead, feeling the weight of her daughter's secret. On the other end, the sound of Kevin's ragged sobbing fills the earpiece.

"I'm sorry, Ms. Ruby… I'm just…"

"I know you're hurting," she says, though there is little pity in her heart. "But the best thing you can do is learn to live without her. If she wants to speak to you, she'll find you. Until then, work on yourself. Goodnight, Kevin."

She hangs up before he can protest. In the dark kitchen of the house Nia just fled, Kevin's grief curdles into a black, oily rage. He realizes Ms. Ruby knows exactly where Nia is. He feels played. In a burst of violence, he hurls his glass against the wall. The Johnnie Walker splashes like a bloodstain, and shards of glass spray across the linoleum.

He buries his face in his hands, let out a dry, jagged laugh. "You think you can leave me without permission? Bitch, you got another thing coming. You watch. I'll find you."

He grabs the scotch bottle by the neck and stumbles into the living room. Above the fireplace sits a framed photo of them at a party two years ago—Nia looking radiant, their arms interlocked in a lie of happiness. He traces her silhouette with a trembling finger.

"You can run," he whispers to the glass, "but you can't hide."

He starts up the stairs, taking a heavy swig of scotch and humming the haunting melody of The Delfonics' *Ready or Not.* He won't be made a fool.

The train lets out a weary groan as it slows, the brakes squealing against the tracks as it pulls into the Detroit station at 7:34 AM. Nia wakes up just as the conductor announces their arrival. She wipes the sleep from her eyes, feeling a strange, hollow lightness in her chest—the "release" from the restroom earlier still lingering as a calm after-effect.

As she steps onto the platform, the air is sharper here, smelling of cold metal and rain. She scans the bustling crowd for Janet's familiar face. She pulls out her phone to call her, but as she hangs up, her heart drops into her stomach.

A man who looks exactly like Kevin—the same build, the same aggressive gait—is charging through the crowd toward her like a raging bull.

Nia freezes. Her lungs seize. She closes her eyes tight, bracing for the impact, for the screaming, for the hand around her arm. But there is no impact. She opens her eyes just in time to see the man breeze past her, murmuring a polite "Excuse me" as he rushes into the arms of a woman standing behind her.

Nia exhales a breath she didn't know she was holding. Her knees feel like water. She grabs her red suitcase and finds a seat by a large window, her hands shaking as she calls home.

The conversation with her parents is a whirlwind. Ms. Ruby tells her about Kevin's 3:00 AM meltdown, and then Charlie hops on the line to give his own, much more colorful version of how he told Kevin off. Nia feels a pang of guilt for the chaos she left behind, but it's drowned out by the knowledge that she finally broke the cycle.

"NIA!"

The voice cuts through the station noise, getting louder by the second just after getting off the phone. Nia turns to see Janet Waters striding toward her, looking like she stepped off a runway.

"Is that my girl Nia with those big ass thighs?" Janet shouts, her arms wide.

Nia laughs, standing up to meet her. Janet is the perfect counterweight to Nia's grounded nature—outgoing, flashy, and fiercely confident. They've been inseparable since first grade in Memphis. While Nia stayed local, Janet took a basketball scholarship to CMU and built a life as a successful counselor for troubled adults in Detroit.

At 6'1", Janet is a force of nature. Her jet-black hair, marked by a distinguished streak of grey at the temple, flows down her back. She wraps Nia in a hug that feels like a fortress. It's the kind of embrace that tells Nia she doesn't have to be strong for a little while.

"Come on, girl. Let's get you out of here," Janet says, grabbing one end of the red bag.

They walk out to Janet's car—a sleek, black 2020 BMW X2. As they pull away from the station, the reality of the situation finally settles on Nia. She has her dignity, a hundred and fifty dollars, and one suitcase.

"How was the trip? I know you picked up at least five numbers," Janet says, navigating the Detroit traffic with one hand.

"Men are the last thing on my mind, Jan," Nia says, looking out at the sprawling city. "I need a job. I need a life."

Her eyes land on a book sliding across the leather back seat: *Being a Better YOU! My Wealth, My Life, My Struggle.* She picks it up, reading the blurb. "Interesting. Yours?"

Janet glances over. "Yeah. Sometimes I need something to stimulate my mind besides dick. I actually bought that for you. It helped me stop caring about other people's opinions and start channeling my own wants."

"Thanks," Nia murmurs, clutching the book to her chest. "I need to start somewhere."

They pull into the driveway of Janet's brick-and-siding townhouse. Inside, Janet leads her to a bright, airy guest room. Nia heaves her luggage onto the bed, the springs protesting with a loud *boing.*

"Thanks for this, Jan. Really."

“Girl, please. I’m just happy you’re away from that asshole.” Janet leans against the doorframe, her phone suddenly vibrating. “Work. I gotta take this. And hey—put that thing in a Ziplock bag or you’ll get a yeast infection!” She points toward Nia’s open suitcase and disappears into the hall.

Nia looks down. In the chaos of travel, her eight-inch, chocolate-colored dildo had wiggled out of its case and was lying prominently on top of her folded jeans. She sighs, picking it up and sitting on the edge of the bed. She smacks the silicone against her palm, a small, triumphant smile playing on her lips. She did it. She’s here.

The transition wasn't easy, but in two months Nia is a hustler. After blasting her resume out like a pimp on a mission and Janet pulling every string she had, Nia landed a dream role: Lead Editor at Brice Publishing, a Fortune 500 magazine focusing on urban art.

She has her own apartment now, a cozy space with a view of the revamped Motor City skyline. Her degree, which Kevin always called a "waste of time," has become her greatest weapon. She’s even started teaching weekend seminars for extra cash.

She sends some of that money back to Memphis to help her parents, but she's careful. She uses an alias and a P.O. Box. She knows Kevin is still out there, lurking in the shadows of her old life, but for the first time in thirteen years, Nia Jefferson is looking forward to the morning.

# CHAPTER IV

## Prey Finding His Cougar

A year has passed since Nia made Detroit her sanctuary, and the city has been good to her. Her career at Brice Publishing is on a steep, steady incline toward success. Her personal life, however, hasn't quite followed the same trajectory. At forty-three, Nia isn't necessarily looking for a soulmate or a white picket fence—she just wants someone to grab a drink with and, more importantly, a reliable, world-class fuck. A "friend with benefits" who actually delivers on the benefits.

She's waded into the dating pool a few times, but each venture has taken a nose dive straight to hell. Sometimes it's her past acting as a psychic roadblock; other times, she realizes she's rushing toward the bedroom just to feel something. Usually, she uncovers a red flag—a hidden wife, a shaky bank account, or a personality like sandpaper—and ends up back on her velvet sofa in oversized sweatpants. There, with her breasts hanging free and a pint of salted caramel ice cream in hand, she yells at the screen during *Love After Lockup*.

When the frustration peaks, "Big Larry"—the heavy, chocolate-toned dildo in her nightstand—is the only one who doesn't disappoint. But Larry doesn't have a heartbeat, and Nia is beginning to miss the warmth of the real thing.

To channel that restless energy, she's intensified her workouts. The "Hot Girl Summer" events at Hart Plaza are approaching, and this cougar is determined to be the sleekest predator in the park.

The morning is brisk, the kind of cold that turns her breath into white plumes of steam. Nia is mid-run, her heart hammering a rhythmic beat against her ribs. She stops at a rusted parking meter to check her vitals, her chest heaving under her moisture-wicking gear.

The silence of the morning is shattered by the screech of tires. A baby-blue Bentley, stylish and wildly out of place on this gritty stretch, jerks to a halt in the middle of the road. One by one, cars begin to pile up behind it, a chorus of impatient horns blaring like a New York traffic jam. The passenger window of the Bentley glides down. An older man leans over the seat, his eyes fixed on Nia's five-foot-four, caramel-skinned frame. He's wearing a crisp white dress shirt, a grey vest, and a black tie, his shoulder-length permed hair slicked back. His face is a map of deep lines, a forehead that looks like it's lived through several eras of history.

Nia ignores the spectacle, focusing on the pulsing numbers on her watch. She hears the shouting of the drivers behind him, but the man doesn't budge. He finds a nearby opening and slides the Bentley into a spot right next to her.

Nia keeps her earbuds in, but the volume is low enough to hear him cupping his hands. "Excuse me, Ma'am! EXCUSE ME!"

She doesn't turn. She places her fingers against the side of her neck, counting her pulse. *Pop-pop-pop-pop.* The man honks his horn—two sharp, annoying blasts. Nia finally yanks an earbud out and fixes him with a look of pure, unadulterated annoyance.

"How you doing, BEAUTIFUL?" he says, flashing a wide grin that reveals a prominent gold tooth.

"Shit," Nia mutters under her breath.

“I was driving to work,” he continues, leaning out the window, “and I was just taken back by your stunning beauty. I was wondering if—”

Nia holds up a hand, cutting him off mid-sentence. “Let me guess. You were wondering if you could take me to dinner? Then we go back to your place so we can 'get to know each other' and you can try to slip more than just a line into me, right?”

She steps closer to the car, her shadow falling across his lap. The man’s grin widens; he thinks he’s winning. He thinks the "hard to get" phase is over. He’s wrong.

“I’m going to cut to the chase, Jerome,” she says, leaning in just enough for him to see the lack of humor in her eyes. “I’m not interested. You’ve got a nice car, a nice suit, and probably a nice career, but right now, I’m just focused on finishing my workout. Have a good day.”

She turns her back and begins to walk away, feeling like she just dropped a mic on the asphalt. There’s a beat of stunned silence, and then the hurricane hits.

“Bitch! You’re missing out on the best thing in your life! Jerome Coffman didn’t need you anyway!” he bellows, his face turning a shade of purple that almost matches his car. He slams the window up and peels back into traffic.

"Oh, so his name is Jerome Coffman? Pleased to meet your miserable ass," Nia says to the empty air, hoisting her middle finger toward his retreating bumper.

She laughs, the sound echoing off the buildings. She doesn't have "bitch" on her birth certificate, but she's been called worse by better men. She pops her earbud back in, cranks the volume, and jogs her forty-two-year-old ass toward the greenery of Belle Isle.

By Tuesday, the adrenaline from the Jerome encounter has faded into a dull, familiar ache for real companionship. After her morning loop around the island, Nia stops at Leo's, a hole-in-the-wall coffee shop that smells of roasted beans and cinnamon.

She's a sweaty mess—black sweat jacket, yoga pants, and pink/white Nike Air Maxes to keep it spicy. A sharp wind whistles through the door as she enters, sending a shiver down her damp spine.

"Hey, Nia! The usual Green Tea Latte?" Corey, the co-owner, calls out from behind the counter.

"You got it. Thanks, CeCe," Nia replies, wiping sweat from her forehead with a towel.

She grabs an abandoned art section of the newspaper and slides into a chair at the end of the counter, her body humming with post-run exhaustion. She's scanning an article when the door chimes.

Her internal radar, dormant for months, suddenly pings with a violent intensity.

A man walks in. He's tall—six-two, at least—with a tone, athletic build draped in a wool vest, a sharp tie, and polished black shoes. His skin is a rich, smooth caramel, and his salt-and-pepper hair is cut into a perfect low fade. His goatee is trimmed tight, flecked with just enough grey to make Nia's pulse skip a beat.

*He looks delicious,* Nia thinks, quickly burying her face behind the newspaper as he walks toward the refrigerator to grab a water. *And I look like a hot, sweaty disaster.* She watches him through the gap in the pages. He's poised, calm. He pays Corey, then tilts his head toward Nia. She freezes, her eyes darting back to the print as if the weather report were the most fascinating thing she'd ever read.

He heads for the exit, then pauses. He changes direction. Nia's heart does a frantic somersault as he pulls out the chair next to her and sits down.

"Hello," he says. His voice is a deep, resonant baritone that vibrates in the air between them. "Foggy day we're having, isn't it?"

He extends a hand. Nia takes it, her skin buzzing against his. "Umm... yeah. It's a good day."

"Name is LaMarcus Harris. And you are...?"

Nia's mind races. *Is he a serial killer? A debt collector? Or just too good to be true?* She decides to play it safe.

"I'm Pam," she says, offering a quick, tight smile. "And it looks like my order is ready."

"Pleased to meet you, Pam," LaMarcus says, his gaze lingering. "I hope I'm not intruding. I'm actually opening a new workout center around the corner called "*Prize Fighter*". We've got state-of-the-art equipment, pools, a sauna, and we specialize in private massage sessions. You should come by the grand opening this week."

He hands her a glossy pamphlet. Nia looks at his face on the cover—he's looking back at her under the slogan "*Today is full of surprises!*"

"I'm new in town and I've been looking for a gym anyway," Nia says, her "Pam" persona gaining confidence. "Sure. Why not?"

She slides her payment to Corey. "Keep the change!"

"Great," LaMarcus says, standing up. He offers a genuine, warm smile. "Hope to see you soon, Pam. Enjoy your day."

He walks out, and Nia stands there for a second, clutching the pamphlet like a winning lottery ticket. Reality hits her—she forgot she isn't Pam. She sees him through the window and waves back with a slightly confused, over-eager look on her face.

On her walk back to the apartment, she passes the storefront for *Prize Fighter*. The windows are covered in brown paper, the muffled sounds of drills and hammers echoing from within. She stares at his picture on the hoarding.

"Yeah," she whispers, taking a long sip of her latte. "I wish he'd surprise me with something long and thick."

She laughs at herself, but as she keeps walking, she knows one thing for sure: Big Larry's days are numbered. It's time for a human touch.

# CHAPTER V

## Slicing And Dicing

Nia pulls open the heavy glass door of her apartment building, catching it just before the latch clicks shut. The lobby smells of floor wax and old radiator heat. She heads for the mailroom, setting her sweating Green Tea Latte and the *Prize Fighter* pamphlet on the polished oak table. As she slides her key into the small brass box, a deep, melodic voice drifts down from the landing.

"Good morning, sunshine!"

Nia turns, a genuine, mile-wide smile lighting up her face. "Good morning, Mr. Mario!"

Mr. Mario descends the stairs with painstaking care, his weight shifting heavily onto a silver-topped cane. He is a man of dignified tragedy—a veteran who sacrificed his youth for a country that eventually turned its back on him. Now, he lives out his exile in Detroit, breathing free but carrying the weight of the family he left behind in Europe.

"I hate to ruin the surprise," he says, his accent thick and rolling, "but the mail carrier left a package at your door while you were out. A nice man brought it—around your age, well-built. A real man. Nothing like that little fucker you used to run the streets with. What was his name? Tiny? Timmy?"

Nia snorts, tucking her mail under her arm. "His name was Brian, Mr. Mario. And you don't have to worry about that little *fucker* coming around here anymore."

"Good riddance!" Mario waves his cane dismissively. "You can do so much better. I bet he was lacking in the department of... how do you say... the measurements?"

Nia laughs, covering her eyes with her palm as she starts up the stairs. "I'd love to stay and chat about Brian's shortcomings, Mr. Mario, I really would! But I've got to get to work. See you later!"

As Nia reaches the top floor, her mood sours instantly. Resting against her door is a clear glass vase filled with an explosion of red roses. Every step closer feel like a stoke of charcoal on her spirit. She knows this play. It was the standard

"Brian Thompson Apology Tour" curriculum. She stops at the door, spotting the "Morton's" label still stuck to the glass, the price tag dangling like a cheap earring.

"This man didn't even take the damn price tag off," she mutters, rolling her eyes so hard it hurts.

She unlocks her door and steps inside, leaving the flowers in the hallway. She sets her coffee and mail on the dining table, trying to ignore the bouquet staring at her from the threshold. After a long beat, she sighs, walks back out, and retrieves the vase, kicking the door shut behind her.

She grabs a cup of water for the thirsty blooms, but as she sets them down, she spots a small envelope tucked between the stems. She pops the seal with a manicured nail and pulls out a card covered in familiar, shaky cursive.

*"My Dearest Nia; I miss you so much. Sorry for all the hurt I gave you! Please forgive me! Love, Brian"*

Nia lets out a sharp, dry laugh that turns into a scoff. She fans the letter in the air once, then flips the lid of the kitchen trash can. The card and the "sorry" roses are unceremoniously dumped into the dark, smelly tomb of coffee grounds and eggshells.

The shower is steaming, the water drumming against the plastic curtain, but Nia is still sitting on the edge of her bed, one shoe off, lost in the memory of why Brian is history.

Four months into the relationship, and things felt... solid. They had traded keys. They were talking about moving in. Nia wanted to play "wife" for a night, so she bought groceries to surprise him at his place after his shift as an operations manager. She had parked across the street, blending into the row of cars, but as she reached for her bags, Brian's car pulled into the drive. Her heart sank—the surprise was spoiled. But then the passenger door opened.

A woman stepped out. Seductive. Tan trench coat, black pumps, shoulder-length hair. Nia's first instinct was to trust him—maybe a sister? A cousin? But as the woman reached the porch, she wrapped her arms around Brian's neck. Brian didn't pull away. He locked lips with her, his hand sliding down to her waist, pulling her flush against him as he kissed her throat. Nia sat in her car, the grocery bags feeling like lead in her lap, watching them vanish inside. She wanted to call Janet. She wanted to burn the house down. Instead, she waited a half hour, her blood turning to ice.

When she finally approached the house, the rain was a cold drizzle. She didn't knock; she used her key and burst through the door like a SWAT team serving a warrant. Brian was on the hardwood floor in the living room, wearing the silk robe Nia had bought him for his birthday. It was open, revealing his oiled-up body. Then she saw it. A male chastity device, complete with a small golden lock.

"Nia!" he yelled, scrambling to his feet. "Baby! What a surprise! What... what are you doing here?"

"What the fuck is *that*?" Nia screamed, pointing at the contraption. "How could you? After everything I told you I went through with my ex... you're behind my back doing this?"

He tried to grab her shoulders, but his robe slipped again, the gold lock glinting in the light. Nia dodged him, ran into the kitchen, and grabbed a heavy chopping knife. She brandished it like a cutlass.

"Baby, put the knife down! We can talk!"

"I'm not putting shit down!" Nia hissed, her eyes darting to the stairs.

She bolted up the steps, Brian stumbling behind her. She burst into the bedroom to find the woman, "Mystique" is her name, standing there stark naked, holding a lit candle. The woman's eyes nearly popped out of her head at the sight of Nia with the blade.

"What is the meaning of this, Brian?" Mystique asked, her voice surprisingly calm as she blew out the candle.

"Explain yourself, nigga!" Nia shrieked. "You have three seconds before I start slicing muthafuckas up!"

Mystique didn't wait. She grabbed her lingerie from the floor and started toward the door. "Lose my number, Brian. And honey," she looked at Nia, "you can do so much better."

Left alone with Brian, Nia listened to his pathetic excuses. "We haven't been clicking... I felt you pushing me away... I met her at work..."

Nia didn't even wait for him to finish. She dropped the knife on the bed, walked out, and slammed the front door so hard the glass cracked. She had cried the whole way home, but the image of Mystique in his car—which the woman had keyed on her way out—brought a dark smile to her face.

The steam in the bathroom is so thick it feels like a physical weight. Nia shakes off the memory and steps into the shower. Her new vertical shower head is a dream, three nozzles pulsing against her caramel skin. She tilts her head back, letting the water massage her scalp, but her mind drifts—not to Brian, but to the man from the coffee shop. LaMarcus.

She imagines his hands, his baritone voice. Her fingers find her nipples, then slide lower, spreading her labia as she begins to work herself into a fever. She's seconds away from the edge, her breathing ragged, when a thunderous pounding hits her front door.

"DAMN IT!" she yells, the fantasy shattering.

The knocking persists. Nia kills the water, throws on her robe, and stalks to the door. She peeks through the hole.

"Who is it?"

"Girl, open the door!"

Nia groans, rolling her eyes as she unbolts the locks. Janet breezes in, taking up the room's energy instantly.

"About time! I thought I was gonna have to call the po-pos!" Janet tosses her coat onto the sofa. She's wearing a dress so tight she can't even cross her legs when she sits.

"I thought you had a meeting," Nia says, leaning against the wall.

"Cancelled! My nineteen-year-old client got arrested for indecent exposure. Showing his business in the park." Janet spots the flowers in the trash. "Brian? Girl, I told you he was trash. Now, his cousin, Jason! That man was hung like a horse. I couldn't walk right for a week!"

Nia perks up. "You fucked Brian's cousin? When?"

"Remember that dinner at Savannah Blue? The dark-skinned brother with the nice teeth? We went back to his place. I checked his medicine cabinet—always check for crazy pills, Nia—and when I came out, he was butt-naked with some Timberlands on. Some real thug out shit! It took a lot of lube just to fit the head in!"

Nia laughs, her irritation fading. "Jesus, Janet. You've seen the light."

"I gave him the whole tour. Mouth, hand, front door, back door surprise... the works. We saw each other for a bit, but he moved to Vegas to run his uncle's shop. I can't do the long-distance relationship. I need that physical interaction—morning, noon, night, and twice on Sundays."

Janet stands up, smoothing her dress. "Anyway, I didn't come here to talk about Jason's jumbo jet. You look like you need to get out. Let's go shopping. My treat."

Nia looks at her messy apartment and the project on her desk. "I don't know, Jan..."

"No excuses. Let's find you some 'fuck-me' pumps and get out of this house." Janet grabs Nia's arm and pulls her toward the bedroom. "Move it!"

# CHAPTER VI

## Meeting In the Dressing Room

"Excuse me, may I see this in a size 9? Please and thank you!" Janet calls out to a store associate with the name "Mark" on the name tag at Kacey's Department Store at Winterplace Mall.

Mark is a lean, middle-aged gentleman with a light complexion and a face that's easy on the eyes. He stands just a bit taller than Janet, offering a polite nod before disappearing through the heavy velvet curtains of the stockroom. Janet leans back in the cushioned chair next to Nia, picking up the display pump and inspecting the heel with the focus of a diamond appraiser.

"I must admit, I really needed this time away from the house," Nia says, letting her shopping bags slump onto the floor. She's been debating whether to tell Janet about her morning encounter at the coffee shop, but the lighthearted energy of the day finally coaxes it out of her. "So, after my run this morning, I saw this guy at the shop. My eyes were locked on him like white on rice."

"Oh yeah? Is he white or black?" Janet asks, already reaching for a strappy sandal on the nearby table.

Nia's face scrunches up. "Does it matter?"

"Not really, but it never hurts to mix up your flavors, honey."

"He's a brotha," Nia says, shaking her head with a smirk. "Anyway, he stopped over and chatted with me about his new business. He gave me a pamphlet and told me to check out his grand opening."

Janet stops mid-reach, her eyes narrowing with recognition. "Wait a minute. You're not talking about that gym opening down the street from you? The one with that fine-ass man plastered on the window?"

Nia's smile is all the confirmation Janet needs.

"The very one," Nia says. "You know him?"

"I don't know that man personally, but I sure wanted to know him before my girl decided she was looking to ride this pony!" Janet laughs, raising her arm and swirling her wrist in the air.

Mark returns then, carrying a stack of boxes. He offers a smooth apology for the wait as he kneels before Janet. He reaches for her leg with practiced grace. Janet slides her foot out of her shoe and into Mark's hand. Instead of just sliding the pump on, Mark begins a slow, firm massage of her arches and toes. Nia blinks, leaning back. She's never seen this level of "customer service" in a department store before.

Janet and Mark's eyes lock. It's as if he's sliding a glass slipper onto a black Cinderella. Janet stands up, modeling the pumps with an executive strut, checking her reflection in the floor-level mirrors.

"Yes, I'll take these," Janet decides, returning to her seat. She places a hand on Mark's shoulder, her fingertips trailing down to his elbow, where she taps him three times.

Mark looks up, catches the signal, and asks a coworker to cover the floor. The coworker gives a quick "OK" sign, and Mark stands, taking the boxes. "I'll have these at the register when you're ready."

As he turns toward the back, Janet raises her hand like a schoolgirl. "Excuse me? Could you direct me to the ladies' room?"

She looks at Nia with a theatrical wince. "Too much water this morning. My bladder is on ten!"

Nia nods, pulling out her phone to open Candy Cruiser. She watches Janet follow Mark behind the curtains. It strikes her as odd—the public restrooms are right by the elevators—but she shrugs it off and starts matching digital candies.

"Quick, we only have a moment," Janet whispers, but Mark is already there, his tongue meeting hers in a hungry tangle. He moves like an octopus, his hands exploring every curve of her body. He peels off her blazer while Janet's hands dive into his slacks, popping the button and dragging the zipper down. His pants hit his knees, and the release is immediate. Janet's eyes roll back as Mark trails kisses down her neck, finding every sensitive spot she possesses.

Outside, Nia is bored. She finishes her game and starts browsing the *Prize Fighter* website. She feels a strange flutter in her stomach—the thrill of the hunt. She's always been the one pursued, but something about Detroit is making her want to take the lead.

"What is taking this girl so long?" Nia mutters. She dials Janet's phone.

A muffled vibration buzzes from the chair next to her. Janet left her purse. Nia sighs, stands up, and walks over to the counter where the other associate is folding socks.

"Excuse me, my friend went to the back to use the restroom and hasn't come back. Is everything okay?"

The salesman looks at the closed backroom door, then back at Nia. "You can go back and knock, ma'am. It's slow. I'll watch your bags."

Nia walks through the curtains and approaches the bathroom door. She's about to call Janet's name when she hears it: a series of rhythmic grunts and a frantic, hushed "Oh shit" from two different voices. Her curiosity wins. She turns the knob—it's unlocked—and edges the door open just an inch. Through the mirror, she sees Janet, braced against the hand dryer, her dress hiked to her waist. Mark is behind her, his work shirt pinned back, giving her his full attention. Janet's expression is one of pure, unholy possession.

Nia should leave. She should walk away. Instead, she finds herself pushing the door open and stepping inside, locking it behind her. Janet's eyes fly open, catching Nia's reflection.

"Really, girl?" Nia says, her voice a mix of shock and amusement.

"Girl, don't go scaring a bitch when she's about to come!" Janet pants, thrusting back against Mark.

Nia watches, her own pulse quickening at the raw, unapologetic energy in the room. This is the "something different" she's always wondered about. Janet reaches out, grabbing Nia's wrist and pulling her hand toward her chest. Nia hesitates for a split second before her fingers find Janet's skin. She begins to flick and rub, leaning in until her lips meet Janet's. Mark, caught in the middle of this unexpected heat, groans as he hits his limit. Pulling away jest before he explodes as Janet collapses against the wall, breathless.

Nia stands back, her heart racing. She's never been part of something so reckless. She looks at Mark, who is leaning against the tiles, catching his breath.

"Wait," Nia says, her voice low. She looks at Janet, who gives her a knowing smirk.

Nia drops to her knees and it's Christmas for Mark. She wraps her hand around his length, stroking him until the veins pop, her eyes fixed on his as she leans in. Janet joins in, teasing his nipples and blowing cool air across his skin.

"I'm about to come, again!" Mark gasps, his head thudding against the wall.

Nia doesn't stop. She picks up the pace, her mouth working in tandem with her hand. When he finally peaks, a jet of white liquid shoots into the air, splashing onto the floor. Mark is completely drained, a look of stunned disbelief on his face.

Nia stands up, wiping her lips and washing her hands at the sink. "I'm going to go let you two clean up."

Ten minutes later, Janet emerges from the back, looking perfectly polished. Mark follows, ringing up the shoes with a grin wider than a four-lane highway.

"That'll be $75.73," Mark says, winking at Janet.

They leave the store, the afternoon sun hitting their faces. They drive to The Jojoba Café off of fourteen mile and Woodard, a quiet spot overlooking the river.

"I hope you're not trying to fuck the waitress to get our lunch for free," Nia teases as they slide into a booth.

"Girl, bye! Mark and I have been friends for years. It's a benefits thing. We look out for each other." Janet sips her water. "Besides, you weren't complaining when you had him in your mouth, Ms. Nightingale."

Nia laughs, turning her attention to the busy traffic. Suddenly, Janet nudges her hard. "Nia, girl. Good-looking man at three o'clock!"

Nia looks over her shoulder and freezes. It's LaMarcus. He's at the counter, but he's already spotted them. He grabs his tea and walks over.

"Hey... Pam, right?" he asks.

"PAM?" Janet echoes, her eyebrows shooting up.

"Actually, it's Nia," Nia says, her cheeks flushing. "I was exhausted this morning. What are you doing over here?"

"Investor meeting," he says, smiling. He meets Janet, and within seconds, Janet is playing matchmaker, mentioning Nia's "tight back" and her need for a "remote massage."

LaMarcus hands them his cards, his eyes lingering on Nia. He starts to leave, then stops and turns back. "I didn't want to be too forward this morning. But if you aren't busy tonight, I'd love to take you to dinner."

Nia freezes. Her mind flickers to her couch and her ice cream. Janet kicks her hard under the table.

"Yes," Nia says quickly. "I'd love to."

LaMarcus beams. "Great. Pick you up at seven?"

Nia writes down her address and watches him walk away, her eyes glued to his backside.

"Girl," Janet says, tapping the table. "Them cheeks got you hypnotized, and I ain't mad at cha."

Nia spends the rest of the afternoon in a daze. She talks to her mother on the phone, omitting the shoe store escapade but gushing about the thirty-three-year-old LaMarcus Harris. As she hangs up, she looks at his card on her dresser.

She lies back on her bed, her eyelids growing heavy. She falls into a deep sleep, her dreams filled with a tall, caramel-skinned man and the promise of a Detroit night that's just beginning.

# CHAPTER VII

## Cherish The Moment

The time strikes 6:00pm when LaMarcus pulls to the curb in his jet-black 2020 Dodge Charger, the engine letting out a low, throaty rumble before he cuts the power. He steps out, looking sharp in a tailored black business suit. He pauses to fasten the middle button of his blazer, smoothing the fabric over his broad shoulders. As he heads toward the entrance, he offers a friendly "Hello" to the neighborhood kids scattered on the front steps before pressing the buzzer for Nia's apartment.

Mr. Mario is in his usual spot, perched in a faded beach chair on the stoop like a sentry. He peers over the rims of his glasses, sizing LaMarcus up with a critical eye.

"Who you here for, young man?" Mario asks, his voice gravelly but firm.

"I'm here for Ms. Jefferson," LaMarcus replies politely, standing his ground. "And you are?"

"A caring neighbor," Mario states sternly. "That's all you need to know."

Nia's voice crackles over the intercom, and a moment later, the buzzer drones, granting him entry. LaMarcus climbs the stairs, his pulse quickening slightly. He finds her door and knocks, straightening his cuffs one last time. When the lock turns and the door swings open, he feels the air leave his lungs.

Nia is a vision in white—a one-shoulder satin dress with a daring slit that reveals the smooth curve of her thigh. Her hair is pinned back elegantly, and her silver three-inch heels show off a fresh, dark pedicure.

Her eyes do a slow crawl over him, taking in the three-piece suit with its subtle silver lining and his polished loafers. He looks clean-shaven, smelling of expensive sandalwood and success. Together, they look like a power couple ready to set Detroit ablaze.

"You look absolutely gorgeous," LaMarcus breathes.

Nia smirks, giving him a playful spin. "Thank you. You're looking pretty handsome yourself."

As they walk out of the building, Mr. Mario's scowl softens into a toothy grin. "Well, well... look who's going to the prom!"

Nia blushes, tucked under LaMarcus's arm. "Thank you, Mr. Mario!"

"Don't you worry, sir," LaMarcus says, catching the old man's eye and gallantly kissing the back of Nia's hand. "She's in good hands."

"You better keep it that way, son!" Mario shouts, playfully shaking his cane at the night sky. "You don't want this old vet hunting you down!"

The atmosphere at "Wright and Company" is electric yet intimate. The overhead lights are dimmed to a warm, romantic amber, highlighting the industrial-chic brick walls and vibrant artwork. Their waiter, Sonny, leads them to a secluded corner table.

"I'll have a glass of water and a 'Sandra,'" Nia tells him, the name of the cocktail sounding like an omen of a good night.

"The same for me on the water," LaMarcus adds, "and a 'One Stone.'"

As they wait for their drinks, the conversation flows with an ease that surprises them both. They talk about Nia's career as an editor—a job she admits she does mostly for the paycheck—and LaMarcus's journey from a wrestling scholarship at Michigan State to spending time in the military to opening his own business.

"California to Michigan? Why the frostbite?" Nia teases, sipping her water.

"Scenery got old," he laughs. "And MSU offered me a path my parents couldn't afford. I took the leap, and I'm glad I did. Besides, the cold weather was worth it if it led to you saying yes this afternoon."

Nia feels her cheeks heat up. By the time the entrees arrive, the "first date" jitters have melted away. They click their glasses, the chime echoing the growing harmony between them.

The drive back is quiet, filled only with the soulful sounds of L.T.D. playing softly through the Charger's speakers. LaMarcus kills the engine in front of her building, but neither moves to leave.

"I had a great time tonight," Nia says softly. "I really like you, LaMarcus. I just... I want to take things slow. That's why I'm not asking you up just yet."

"I respect that," he says, his voice dropping an octave. "If it's right, there's no need to rush. But... can I at least have a kiss?"

Nia doesn't answer with words. She reaches out, her hand tracing the line of his jaw before pulling him in. The kiss is slow, deep, and tastes like fire. For a split second, Nia regrets her "take it slow" rule. Her body is screaming for him to follow her upstairs, but she pulls back, breathless, watching the windows fog up from their shared heat.

A few weeks go by and the honeymoon phase is still going strong, though work has made their time together a rare commodity. Determined to see more of her man and keep her "cougar" physique in check, Nia decides to sign up for a membership at *Prize Fighter*.

The facility is stunning—two stories of state-of-the-art equipment and high ceilings. As Nia surveys the yoga studio, she hears a familiar voice.

"NIA!"

She turns, and for a moment, the world goes into slow motion. LaMarcus is walking toward her in a pair of grey sweatpants and a fitted shirt that leaves nothing to the imagination. The way his muscles move under the fabric has Nia's mouth going dry.

"I'm so glad you stopped by," he says, pulling her into a warm hug and a lingering kiss. "Let me show you around."

"Ya, I have some free time and what to check out the place, maybe see about a membership"

He leads her through the gym, but Nia is barely listening to the specs of the treadmill. She's watching the way he interacts with his clients—patiently helping an elderly woman with a machine, his kindness radiating. She bites her lip, her resolve to stay celibate crumbling by the second.

When they reach his office, he ushers her in and locks the door. The atmosphere shifts instantly. The "professional" mask slips.

"So," Nia says, leaning against his desk as he grabs her a bottle of water. "Let's talk about the... membership packages."

She watches him as he bends over the fridge, the grey fabric of his sweats stretching over his backside. Her leg starts to bounce. She's catching a serious case of hot flashes.

LaMarcus turns around, a price sheet in hand, but his eyes drop to the V-neck of her shirt. The scent of her perfume is doing a number on his self-control. He steps closer to explain the plans, and Nia notices a very prominent, rhythmic nudge against the front of his sweatpants.

"Looks like someone has another option in mind for sealing the deal," she purrs, licking her lips.

LaMarcus looks down, his face flushing. "Oh shit... I'm sorry. I didn't even realize..."

"Don't be sorry," Nia says, reaching out and dragging him toward her by the waistband. "I think it's time we move to the advanced training."

She slides off her chair to her knees, her fingers nimble as she undoes the drawstring. When he's finally exposed, she takes a moment to admire the view. "My... aren't you a hefty fella?"

She doesn't wait for an answer. She takes him in, savoring the taste and the thrill of finally crossing that line.

LaMarcus grips the edge of the desk, his knuckles white as he groans her name.

The office encounter is a blur of heat and pent-up desire. He lifts her onto the chair, leaning it back against the sofa for leverage, his tongue finding her center with a ferocity that has her screaming into the quiet office. When she finally climaxes, her body spasms, a release months in the making.

Eventually, she pulls him into her, their eyes locking with an intensity that speaks of months of restraint finally breaking. As they move together, the rhythm is perfect—a seamless culmination of every late-night talk, every shared look across a dinner table, and the agonizing weight of the waiting.

LaMarcus never breaks the connection, his hands finding her waist as he lifts her into his arms. He guides them through the dim light, walking backward with his lips still pressed fervently against hers. Every step is deliberate until they finally land in the deep, familiar embrace of his leather chair, the muffled creak of the hide lost beneath the sound of their shared breath.

A sudden, booming knock on the door shatters the silence, the sound echoing off the office walls like a gunshot.

"HELLOOO? LAMARCUS? YOU IN THERE?"

The air in the room instantly turns electric with a different kind of tension. LaMarcus freezes, his muscles locking as he presses a warning finger to Nia's lips, his heart hammering against his ribs like a trapped bird.

But Nia doesn't stop. She just grins, a mischievous glint in her eyes as she bites down softly on his finger, continuing her relentless, rhythmic movement on his manhood. The agonizing contrast of the danger outside the door and the heat of her body becomes too much to bear. As Troy's shadow finally shifts and retreats from the hallway, the last of LaMarcus's restraint snaps.

He stifles a groan against her shoulder, his eyes rolling back as a powerful, shuddering orgasm crashes through him. It's an explosive release when he pulls out, leaving him trembling and completely undone. When it's finally over, they are both a beautiful, tangled mess. LaMarcus collapses back into the deep curve of his leather chair, his chest heaving as he gasps for air, the adrenaline and pleasure still humming under his skin.

"You're going to be the death of me," he laughs.

Nia gets off of him and cleans herself up, realizing she's made a mess of her shirt. LaMarcus fumbles through a drawer and tosses her a promotional *Prize Fighter* tee. "Size large? I want to make sure your girls have room."

She pulls the fresh shirt on, the scent of the new fabric mixing with the heat of sex in the room. They seal the deal with one last, lingering kiss.

"I'll call you tonight," Nia says, walking toward the door with a new spring in her step.

As she exits the facility, the Detroit air feels cooler, fresher. She feels like a queen who finally found her kingdom. But as she walks down the neighborhood, a small, nagging chill touches her spine. She's happy, but in the back of her mind, she knows that life has a way of bringing the past back to the surface just when things are getting piece back together.

# CHAPTER VIII

## Returning Home isn't Always Easy

Ms. Ruby was at the dining room table, the sharp *snip-snip* of her scissors through newspaper coupons the only sound in the quiet house. A sudden, heavy pounding at the door made her jump, the scissors clattering onto the wood.

She rose steadily, her knees popping, and smoothed her apron as she moved to the front door. Peering through the narrow side window, her heart sank. It was Kevin. Even through the glass, she could see the "sauce" had a firm grip on him; he looked like a man who had been driven to her doorstep by the bottom of a bottle.

Shaking her head in shame, she cracked the door just far enough for the security chain to snap taut. The smell of stale Scotch wafted in immediately. She glanced at the wall clock…1:14 in the afternoon.

"Aren't you supposed to be at work, boy?" she asked, her voice tight with disapproval.

"Where she at?" Kevin slurred. His eyes were bloodshot, his stance a dangerous, swaying tilt.

"Who the hell are you talking about?"

"Who am I talking about?" Kevin's voice rose to a roar. "Your damn *daughter*! Where the hell is she?"

Before Ms. Ruby could draw breath to answer, Kevin threw his weight against the door. The wood groaned, and the security chain snapped like a piece of dry string. Ms. Ruby fell backward, her small frame hitting the hardwood floor with a sickening thud.

Kevin stumbled into the living room, one arm catching the back of the sofa to keep from collapsing. "NIA!" he screamed toward the ceiling.

In the backyard, Charlie was deep into the guts of his rebuilt Ford Mustang. When the muffled sounds of a struggle reached him, he didn't hesitate. He tossed his wrench into the metal toolbox with a loud *clang* and wiped his oil-stained hands on a greasy rag, limping toward the back door as fast as his bad leg would carry him. Upstairs, Kevin was a whirlwind of drunken rage, leaning against the beige walls for support as he kicked open closet doors.

"Nia! Get out here!"

Downstairs, Charlie burst through the screen door. "Ruby? Ruby!"

He found her in the front hall, her elderly body trembling as she used the doorknob to haul herself off the floor. His eyes went wide with protective fury just as Kevin came stumbling back down the stairs. Kevin missed the final two steps, pitching forward and sprawling onto the hardwood.

"Where... where's your daughter, old man?" Kevin spat, pushing himself up.

Charlie adjusted his glasses, his face hardening into a mask of stone. He balled his right hand into a fist, the knuckles chalk color.

"Son, did you do this to my wife?"

"I don't want no trouble from you people," Kevin growled, his pores leaking the sharp scent of booze. "I just want her back home!"

Ms. Ruby grabbed Charlie's arm, her fingers digging into his sleeve. She could feel the heat radiating off him—the quiet, dangerous energy of a man pushed too far. "Charlie, don't," she whispered.

He patted her hand gently, then pried her arm away. He stepped toward Kevin, his limp barely noticeable now.

"What the hell is wrong with you, boy? You come into my house, push my wife to the ground, and yell for a woman who left your bitch-ass over a year ago?"

Kevin's eyes blinked rapidly as the truth tried to penetrate the fog of alcohol. "Where is Nia?" he demanded, trying to shove past Charlie into the dining room.

Charlie moved like a veteran guard, blocking the path. "We've dealt with your mess far too long. Face it, son. She's gone. She ain't *never* coming back to you."

Kevin stopped. He looked down at the floor, his fingertips tracing the rim of a tall green glass vase resting on a nearby stand.

"She doesn't love you," Charlie continued, his voice low and cutting. "You ain't shit, and—"

The snap was instantaneous. Kevin's sanity evaporated. He lunged, grabbing the neck of the vase and swinging it in a wide, violent arc.

*CRACK.*

Green shards of glass exploded into the air, sparkling like emeralds in the afternoon light. Charlie's head snapped to the side, and his body followed, hitting the floor with a heavy, lifeless *thud.* His feet twitched in a rhythmic, terrifying response to the trauma.

"CHARLIE!" Ms. Ruby shrieked, throwing herself over her husband's body to protect him from another blow. Kevin stood over them, his eyes empty, still clutching the jagged neck of the broken vase.

"Kevin, what have you done?" Ruby sobbed, checking Charlie's vitals. "Call 911! Hurry!"

Stung by the sight of the blood pooling on the hardwood, Kevin dropped the glass and bolted. He scrambled out the door, jumped the porch steps, and tore away in his car, his tires kicking up a cloud of grey gravel.

Ruby reached for the house phone, her hands shaking so violently it took two tries to lift the receiver. "911, what's your emergency?"

"Please come quick!" she cried into the line, her eyes fixed on Charlie's shallow, ragged breathing. "My husband is dying!"

Nia was mid-presentation on a Zoom call, her screen filled with editorial layouts, when her phone buzzed. *Ms. Ruby.* She tapped "ignore," sending it to voicemail. She couldn't stop now. But when the phone rang again five minutes later, a cold pit formed in her stomach. Ms. Ruby never called twice unless the world was ending.

"Hey, Ms. Ruby, what's going on?" Nia asked, shutting her laptop.

"It's your father. He's heading to the hospital. We need you here, Nia."

"Wait... what happened?"

"KEVIN," Ruby spat, her voice a cocktail of grief and lethal anger. "That's what happened. If I get my hands on that boy..."

Nia doesn't hear the rest. Her vision blurs as the room seems to tilt on its axis. In the sudden, ringing silence of her mind, the ghosts she thought she buried come screaming back.

The sound of the television or the hum of the fridge fades, replaced by the memory of Kevin's voice—sharp, jagged, and cruel. She can still hear the way he used to dismantle her piece by piece, the way he hurt her family with words that cut deeper than any blade. She thought she had outrun that history, that she had built a fortress of a life that his shadow couldn't penetrate. But now, just as she is finally standing on her own two feet, the old familiar dread coils in her gut like a snake.

Within the hour, the heavy silence is broken by the frantic turn of a key. Janet and LaMarcus are at her door. Janet throws the door open for LaMarcus, who doesn't hesitate. He runs straight to Nia, his boots thudding against the hardwood until he reaches her, pulling her into an embrace that smells of safety and expensive cologne. Against the warmth of his chest, the echoes of Kevin's voice begin to dim, but the fear remains—a cold reminder that the past is never as far behind as she wants it to be.

Nia finally broke, her muffled cries disappearing into his chest. "He's stable," she sobbed, "but he's got a broken wrist and a head injury. He landed wrong when he fell."

"Have they caught the bastard yet?" LaMarcus asked, his jaw set tight.

"Chile," Janet said from the loveseat, "those Memphis officers are country bumpkins. They move at their own speed, which is slow as hell."

Nia pulled back, wiping her eyes. "I'm catching the 7:00 PM flight to Memphis."

LaMarcus checked his watch. 3:46 PM. "Good. That gives me enough time to shower and pack."

Nia looked at him, stunned. "You don't have to come, baby. I'll be okay."

"I know you'll be okay," he said, kissing her forehead. "I just want to be there for support. I'll be back in an hour."

Janet watched him leave, then leaned toward Nia. "Chile... does he come in a twin pack? Because I need some of *that*."

The flight to "Grind City" was a blur of anxiety. When they landed, the large "Welcome to Memphis" sign felt less like a greeting and more like a warning.

At the car rental counter, they were met by a familiar face—Thomas Morrison, an old high school classmate of Nia's. After some clumsy typing and shaking crumbs out of a keyboard, Thomas realized who he was talking to.

"Nia Jefferson? From Ridgecrest High?" Thomas grinned, showing off a prominent yellow front tooth. "Last I heard, you and Kevin were heavy into each other!"

"Ancient history, Tom," Nia said, pointedly taking LaMarcus's hand.

After they left with their keys, Thomas picked up the desk phone. He waited for the second party to answer.

"Kevin speaking."

"Yo, Kevin. It's Tom. Guess who's back in town renting a car?"

Kevin's eyes widened. "Don't play with me, Tom. Who?"

"Nia. And she brought a guest. A man. A real good-looking one, too. Looks like she upgraded, buddy."

Kevin slammed the phone down, the smirk on his face turning into a mask of pure malice. He called for his assistant, Barbara, the secret woman in Kevin's crumbling life.

"Reschedule my appointments," Kevin barked, grabbing his coat. "I'm leaving early."

Nia and LaMarcus pulled into Ms. Ruby's driveway at 10:25 PM. The air was thick with the mouth-watering scent of hickory-smoked baby back ribs.

"Damn," LaMarcus said, sniffing the air. "If Memphis is popping like this at night, I might need to relocate."

"Just get the bags, Rib-boy," Nia teased, though her heart was heavy as she knocked on the screen door.

The reunion was bittersweet. Ms. Ruby ushered them in, nearly fainting when she realized LaMarcus wasn't a taxi driver but Nia's man. "Boy, bring yourself over here and give Ms. Ruby a hug! You feel like your daddy did back when he came home from the war!"

Outside in the shadows, Kevin watched from his car. He snapped photos of them on his phone and scribbled down the license plate of their rental car. He called Barbara.

"I'm sending you some photos and a plate number. Run a background check on this guy. I want to know everything. Also, call Robert to make a special routine stop on the car.

"On it, baby!" Barbara whispered, already plotting.

Inside, the atmosphere was lighter. Ms. Ruby had laid out a spread of ribs, mac and cheese, and yams. LaMarcus ate like he was trying to win a trophy.

"So, Ms. Ruby," Nia asked over herbal tea. "They still haven't caught Kevin?"

"Chile, he knows everyone in this town. The police are brushing it under the rug."

Nia sighed. "I think we're gonna turn in, Ms. Ruby. The dinner was amazing, but I'm exhausted." She moved to unfasten her pants button to breathe.

"Good idea," Ms. Ruby said, shuffling toward the stairs. "Nia, get LaMarcus a blanket for the couch."

Nia stopped. "Ms. Ruby, I'm over forty years old. I think I'm old enough to have a guest in my room."

Ms. Ruby turned on the stairs, her expression dropping into a look of sheer authority. She walked back down and grabbed both of their wrists, inspecting their ring fingers.

"Just as I suspected. No rings. In the Book of Ruby, you are both single. If anyone is gonna be sleeping with someone in this house, you're looking at her!" She wagged a finger in the air. "And if anyone is gonna be *fucking* under this roof, you're looking at her, too! GOODNIGHT!"

Nia looked at LaMarcus, who was staring at the small, stiff, green French sofa with a look of genuine concern.

"I'm sorry, baby," Nia whispered, kissing him. "You know how she is."

"It's okay, love," LaMarcus sighed, testing the rock-hard cushion. "I just hope I can fit on this thing."

"Have fun with that," Nia teased, heading up the stairs.

LaMarcus sat on the edge of the sofa, untying his shoes as the silence of the Memphis night settled in. "This is going to be a long night," he muttered to the empty room.

# CHAPTER IX

## Midnight Delight

It is the wee hours of the morning, and Nia is losing the battle with her own mind. She tosses and turns, the cotton sheets tangling around her legs like vines. Every time she closes her eyes, she's back in that living room, a silent witness to Kevin's shadow looming over her father.

Outside, a restless breeze picks up, sending a sudden gust to rattle the windowpanes. A stray tree branch scrapes against the siding with a rhythmic, skeletal *scratch-scratch-scratch* that jars her fully awake. She stares up at the darkened ceiling, her heart hammering a frantic beat against her ribs. Sweat beads on her forehead, trickling into her hairline.

"If I can't sleep," Nia whispers to the empty room, her voice raspy, "I might as well do something to earn the rest."

She sits up, her Aqua Scooby-Doo nightshirt bunching around her waist. The air in the room is heavy and humid, making her skin feel hypersensitive. She traces a hand over her chest, feeling the tension coiled in her muscles like a spring. She realizes then, with a pang of frustration, that in the chaos of the move and the emergency, she forgot to pack "Big Larry"—her usual remedy for nights like this.

Desperate for a distraction to quiet the hum of anxiety in her blood, she slides out of bed. Her slipper socks muffle her footsteps as she creeps toward the door. She eases it open, the hinges giving a tiny, treacherous moan that makes her freeze. Silence follows, save for the steady, rhythmic snoring of Ms. Ruby coming from the room down the hall.

Nia sneaks past her mother's door, trailing her fingers along the hallway wallpaper to steady her balance in the dark. She navigates the stairs like a ghost, skipping the third step from the bottom—the one she knows has a loud, piercing creak.

As she rounds the corner into the living room, she sees him. LaMarcus is sprawled on the cramped French sofa, a study in unconscious grace. The fleece blanket has slipped to his waist, exposing the broad, caramel expanse of his chest, shimmering with a fine sheen of sweat from the Southern heat.

He's improvised for his height by propping his legs up on two kitchen chairs tucked against the end of the couch.

"He looks so peaceful," Nia murmurs to herself, her eyes tracing the muscular line of his arm tucked behind his head. "And way too delicious to ignore."

She crawls toward the sofa like a panther scoping its prey, the hardwood cool against her knees. Sliding under the blanket, she finds he's discarded his underwear in the heat. The sight of him, relaxed and ready, is the only thing that has made her feel grounded since she touched down in Memphis.

She leans in, her breath warm against his skin. She starts with soft, grazing kisses that eventually deepen into a slow, deliberate rhythm. LaMarcus's breathing hitches, shifting from the steady drone of sleep to a sharp, ragged intake of air.

"Yeah, baby… you know I like that," he mumbles, his voice thick with sleep, a faint snore following the words as if his body is responding while his mind is still drifting. Nia smiles against him, working with a focused intensity. She gags slightly, the sound echoing in the quiet room. She freezes, her eyes darting toward the stairs, terrified of hearing her mother's footsteps. The thought of Ms. Ruby catching them in the middle of the "Guest Room" rules would be a death sentence.

When no one moves upstairs, Nia regains her courage. She pulls her nightshirt over her head, letting the moonlight through the curtains silver her bare skin. She straddles his legs, facing away from him, and guides him in.

"5, 4, 3, 2, 1… blast off," she thinks, a jagged breath escaping her as she settles down.

The friction and the heat finally pull LaMarcus out of the fog. He blinks, his eyes adjusting to the sight of Nia's arched back and the rhythmic movement of her hips. He reaches out, his large hands finding purchase on her waist to steady her.

"Don't say a word," Nia whispers, leaning back until her head rests on his chest. "Just give me this."

They move in a silent, desperate harmony. Nia watches their shadows dance on the wall, her climax hitting her like a freight train, leaving her shivering and spent.

Eventually, they migrate to the floor, spreading the fleece blanket over the rug for more room. The birds are just beginning their early morning chatter when they finally finish, lying limb-to-limb in the cooling air.

"You should probably get back upstairs," LaMarcus whispers, kissing her damp forehead. "Before your Ms. Ruby finds us ass-naked on her good rug."

Nia stumbles to her feet, her legs feeling like Jell-O. LaMarcus tosses her the Scooby-Doo shirt, and she disappears up the stairs just as the first rays of sun hit the porch. By 8:57 AM, the smell of sizzling bacon wafts into Nia's room, acting like smelling salts. she washes up, dresses in fresh clothes, and heads down to the kitchen. Ms. Ruby is at the sink, laughing at something LaMarcus is saying as he whisks eggs with practiced ease. The tension from the night before has vanished from the room, replaced by the domestic clatter of breakfast.

"Good morning, all," Nia says, grabbing a piece of toast.

"Morning, honey," Ms. Ruby beams. "Your man here is a natural in the kitchen."

"I'm just trying to earn my keep, Ms. Ruby," LaMarcus winks at Nia.

The conversation is light until the reality of the day settles back in. Ms. Ruby wipes a stray tear with a floral towel. "You know, this is the first time since Charlie got back from

Korea that we haven't slept in the same room. His snoring drives me crazy, but the quiet was worse."

Nia and LaMarcus exchange a quick, guilty glance, thankful the "quiet" wasn't interrupted by their own late-night activities. The mood shifts when they arrive at the hospital at noon. As they walk through the parking lot, Nia can't shake the feeling of eyes on the back of her neck. She scans the rows of cars for Kevin's familiar vehicle, but sees nothing but sunbaked asphalt.

They find Nia's father in Room 416L. The room is dim and smells of antiseptic. Charlie looks smaller in the hospital bed, his head bandaged and his eye bruised, but his face lights up the moment Nia enters.

"Baby girl!" he rasps, tears welling in his good eye.

Nia rushes to him, mindful of the tubes and wires. After the introductions—and a brief, stern "protective father" interrogation of LaMarcus—Nia notices something on the bedside table. A green glass vase filled with fresh white flowers. She moves to the other side of the bed, her fingers trembling as she pulls the card from the arrangement. She opens it in secret. One word is written in the center: *Sorry.*

She recognizes the jagged, familiar script. Kevin. Nia's blood runs cold. She bolts to the window, searching the street four stories below. He's been here. He knows where they are. She slips the card into her back pocket, the secret burning against her hip. She doesn't tell a soul—not wanting to ruin the fragile peace of the visit.

That evening, back at the house, Nia's phone rings. It's Janet. Nia retreats to her bedroom to answer. "Girl, you won't believe it," Nia whispers into the receiver. "He left flowers. At the hospital. A note that just said 'Sorry.'"

"Chile, you need to watch your back!" Janet's voice is sharp with worry. "That fool has a few bolts loose. You need to come home to Detroit as soon as your daddy is clear."

"I know," Nia sighs, rubbing her temples. "I just can't leave Ms. Ruby yet."

"Well, hurry up. Even Mr. Mario is missing you—that old man tried to pinch my ass today. I had to slap the varicose veins out of his hand and tell him the merchandise is off-limits!"

Nia laughs, the first real laugh all day. They hang up, and Nia prepares for another night of looking at the ceiling, wondering how much power one man can hold over a town—and her life.

Miles away, Kevin stares at the world through the bottom of a Scotch glass. His house, once filled with the promise of a life with Nia, is now a tomb of unpaid bills and foreclosure notices. His phone rings. It's Barbara.

"She's living in Detroit now," Barbara reports. "Editor for a magazine. The guy was in the military, honorable discharged and owns a gym. They're living a simple life, Kevin. No major debt."

"Ex military," Kevin mutters, the Scotch burning his throat. He hangs up without a thank you. He looks at the only photo of Nia he hasn't smashed yet. The rage is a slow, cold simmer.

In her own home, Barbara puts her phone down, feeling a familiar sting of disappointment. She looks at her fiancé, Ryan, sleeping soundly in the next room. She thinks back to two years ago, the night she first gave in to Kevin on the living room floor—the night she chose excitement over respect. She knows Kevin is spiraling. She knows he's dangerous. But as she stares at her engagement ring, she realizes her loyalty is not with the man next to her.

# CHAPTER X

## If I Can't Have You

Saturday morning arrives with a cruel cheerfulness. A flock of robins' lands on the oak branch right outside Nia's window. Their melodic chirping cutting through the heavy silence of the room. Nia groans, tempted to hurl a shoe at the glass, but she takes it as a divine nudge to wake up after a night spent tossing in a sea of worry. She needs to move. She needs to breathe.

Nia washes up and pulls on her sleek, black jogging outfit. Creeping downstairs, she finds the house still held in a deep slumber; Ms. Ruby and LaMarcus are apparently still "dancing in their individual dreams," the only sound being the soft hum of the refrigerator.

At 8:00 AM, the Memphis air is surprisingly calm. The sun is a pale gold disk, not yet high enough to bake the pavement. As Nia begins a steady jog, the neighborhood feels like a living scrapbook. She passes old, crumbling brick buildings that hold the ghosts of her wilder youth, but the further she runs, the more the landscape shifts. Gentrification is creeping in—shiny new storefronts and modern townhomes are replacing the jagged edges of her memories.

"*Council finally got their pockets filled, I guess*," she breathes out, her sneakers rhythmically hitting the asphalt.

She reaches the site of her old high school, which has since been leveled and turned into a manicured park. She finds a dark green metal bench—right where her eleventh-grade locker used to stand—and sits for a moment. Pigeons flutter down, pecking at imaginary crumbs. For the first time since she landed, the prickle of paranoia on her neck fades. She feels a strange sense of closure, as if she is finally blooming in the light of her new life.

She checks her watch. She needs to get back before the house wakes up. As she jogs down the final stretch toward Ms. Ruby Street, the peace is shattered. A grey Buick, moving in the opposite direction, slows to a crawl. The driver slams it into reverse, the transmission letting out a metallic whine. The car backs up alongside her, forcing her to stop. The dusty-tinted window rolls down with a slow, agonizing creak; It's Kevin.

He looks like a man who has been pickled in Scotch. His skin is ashy, his eyes bloodshot and sunken, and his beard is a patchy mess of stubble and razor bumps. He looks ten years older than the man she left. In the backseat, open bottles of Johnnie Walker sit where Nia once imagined a car seat for the child they lost. The smell drifting from the car is a nauseating cocktail of vomit, stale cigarettes, and fried chicken.

"Did Daddy get my flowers?" Kevin rasps, before letting out a wet, rattling cough into his hand.

Nia's throat constricts. She looks around the empty street, praying for a witness. "What do you want, Kevin?" she asks, crossing her arms tightly.

"My, my... look at little Nia," he sneers, his golden front tooth catching the light as he smiles. "All grown up and full of confidence. Well, I came for what's rightfully mine. *You.*"

"I'm nobody's property," Nia says, a sharp, cold laugh escaping her.

His expression sours instantly. He kills the engine and pushes open the rusted, squeaky door. Nia takes a reflexive step back as he looms over her, his body odor hitting her like a physical blow. He leans in close, his voice a dangerous hiss.

"What did you say to me, woman?" He giggles to himself, a sound that chills her to the bone. He reaches out and presses a finger to her temple, his eyes dark and hollow. "I *own* you, bitch! You don't run this town, and you sure as hell don't run me. That boy at Ms. Ruby's house. The one you play house with! He's a dead man if he isn't out of here by sundown. And you're next."

He backs into his car without another word. The Buick jerks forward, tires spitting gravel into the air as he disappears around the corner.

Nia doesn't run; she walks, her legs feeling like lead. She enters the house and slams the door with a force that vibrates through the floorboards. Ms. Ruby and LaMarcus burst out of the kitchen, their faces pale with alarm.

"Nia? What happened?" LaMarcus reaches for her, but she pushes him back, her chest heaving as the first sob breaks through.

Then, she collapses into his arms, a guttural scream of frustration and fear escaping her. They guide her to the couch, where she weeps until her eyes are swollen. She tells them she saw Kevin, but she keeps the death threats locked behind her teeth, terrified of what Ms. Ruby or LaMarcus might do.

Ms. Ruby reaches for the phone, her face set in a grim line. "I'm calling the police."

"No!" Nia cries, grabbing her mother's wrist. "Don't. They won't help, Ms. Ruby. He says he runs things. Just... put it down. Please."

Reluctantly, Ruby hangs up. A strange, quiet resolve settles over the older woman. She grabs her purse and Charlie's keys. "I'm heading to the market," she says flatly. "I'll be back."

"I'll go with you," LaMarcus offers, but Ruby shakes her head.

"You stay here. Comfort my daughter. She needs you more than I do."

Once the door clicks shut, the house feels too big. Nia looks at LaMarcus, her voice trembling. "Kevin sent those flowers. There was a note. And today... he told me that if you aren't out of Memphis by sundown, he's going to kill you. Then me."

LaMarcus pulls his hand back, his eyes widening. He rubs his thighs, the silence stretching as rage and sadness flicker across his face.

"I'm so sorry," Nia whispers, reaching for her phone. "I'll get you a flight. You need to leave—"

He pushes the phone away and tilts her chin up. "I'm not going anywhere without you."

He kisses her—a hard, desperate kiss that tastes of salt and survival. It's a spark in a dark room. Nia groans, her fear twisting into a sudden, frantic need for connection. She yanks him to his feet and pulls him toward the stairs.

In her childhood bedroom, she kicks the door shut. The world outside—the threats, the Scotch-breath, the broken vase—disappears. She needs to feel alive. She needs to feel *him*.

They tangle together against the door, a frantic wrestling of denim and cotton. He zips her jacket down, his hands finding the familiar weight of her breasts, and Nia pushes back against him, needing the friction.

"You want this?" he murmurs into her neck.

"Yes," she gasps.

The encounter is raw and urgent. He goes to his knees, his tongue a welcome fire, before she pulls him onto the bed. She straddles him, taking him in with a slow, deep glide that feels like coming home. They lock eyes, their breathing the only sound in the room, until the front door downstairs bangs open.

"I'm back!" Ms. Ruby's voice echoes up the stairs.

LaMarcus freezes, his hands gripping Nia's hips. "Was that your mom?" he whispers, still buried deep inside her.

Nia is too far gone to answer. She hears the *thud-thud* of orthopedic shoes on the stairs. She scrambles off him, heart racing, and cracks the door just as Ms. Ruby reaches the landing.

"Nia? You in there, girl?"

"Yeah, Ms. Ruby," Nia says, her bare side against the door, her skin flushed. "Just... just waking up from a nap. How was the store?"

"Fine, fine. I saw Betty Blinken. She says Sister Mary's son got arrested in Detroit." Ms. Ruby pauses, looking suspicious. "Where's LaMarcus? I didn't see him downstairs."

Behind Nia, LaMarcus isn't stopping. He slides back into her, a slow, silent stroke. Nia gasps, gripping the doorknob until her knuckles turn pale. "He... he went for a walk. Needed some air."

"That's good. He's a respectful man," Ruby says, leaning in as if to peer through the crack.

The doorbell rings downstairs, a miraculous salvation.

"Oh, for heaven's sake," Ruby grumbles. "Go back to sleep, honey. I'll get it."

As soon as the footsteps retreat, Nia closes the door and falls back into the rhythm. It's a game of muffled moans and desperate heat. When the climax finally takes them, LaMarcus covers her mouth with his hand, swallowing her cries of joy into his palm. They collapse into each other, the sweat-slicked silence of the room finally offering the peace the morning had promised.

# CHAPTER XI

## Power In Motion

LaMarcus lies sprawled in the center of Nia's bed, his chest rising and falling in a heavy, rhythmic heave as he recovers from the intensity of their morning. The air in the room is thick and warm, smelling of musk and the lingering heat of their skin. Nia eases the bedroom door open, scanning the quiet hallway like a scout before darting to the bathroom. She returns moments later, clutching two steaming washcloths.

After clicking the door shut, she tosses one cloth onto LaMarcus's bare chest. The wet warmth makes him hiss with a smile as Nia begins to methodically wipe the sheen of their passion from her skin.

"Let me ask you something," LaMarcus says, his voice a low rumble. He catches the cloth and begins cleaning himself.

"After the absolute assault you just put on me? Ask away," Nia replies with a playful, tired smirk.

"Why does your dad call your momma 'Ms. Ruby'?" He sits up, gathering his discarded clothes from the thick carpet.

Nia stops mid-motion, a clean shirt halfway over her head. She takes a long, grounding breath, the weight of the past suddenly filling the room. "The short version? It's out of respect for Claire Davenport—my biological mother."

Nia moves to the closet, sifting through hangers for something fresh. LaMarcus watches her, draping the damp cloth over the wooden headboard. "And the long version? If you're willing to go there."

Nia pulls on clean lace underwear and walks back to the bed, sinking onto the mattress beside him. She pats his thigh, her gaze drifting toward the window, looking past the glass into a history he's never seen.

"Her name is Ruby Dee Jenkins from Clarendon County, SC." Nia begins, her voice soft but steady. "She came from a house that was broken before she was even born. Her mother died when she was two, leaving her with an abusive father and an older brother named Joseph. Joseph was her world. He was her shield, her protector. One night, Joseph and friend got into a fight with a group of older white me. They held their own and ran in the woods. That night, two men kicked in the door and dragged Joseph away while Ruby screamed. Two days later, they found his body floating in the Lake Marion River. Ruby lost her brother, and not long after, she lost her innocence to the hands of the man who she called father."

LaMarcus lies back, the humor gone from his face as he absorbs the truth Nia had pieced together from the dusty journals she found years ago in the attic.

"She hated her name because people always compared her to the actress Ruby Dee," Nia continues, a sad smile touching her lips. "People would crack jokes, asking where Ossie Davis was. It made her feel small, so she became 'Ms. Ruby.' After high school, she was desperate to escape the laundry mats and the waitressing women the city employed women. When her father was shot dead robbing a liquor store, she needed money fast and started dancing."

"Ms. Ruby? Shaking a tail feather?" LaMarcus breathes out, tucking a pillow under his head.

"Dancing got her to Memphis. Her stage name was 'Honeycomb,' on the circuit because every man in Memphis wanted to sting her hive," Nia says, finally pulling up her jeans.

"She met Claire—my real mother—at the club. Claire went by 'Sunshine.' They were best friends, sisters by choice. Then, one night, a soldier named Charlie Jefferson walked in. He fell for Ms. Ruby instantly, but she turned him down. Claire, though... she was a sucker for a man in a uniform."

Nia stands up, pacing the small room as the story unfolds. "Claire found out she was pregnant right after Daddy went back to the army. Ms. Ruby moved in to help her. But here's the thing: Dad kept writing, but Claire never got the letters. When he finally came home with an honorable discharge and flowers in his hand, he found Ms. Ruby holding me. Claire had died from a ruptured vessel during my birth. He was devastated—a single father with a newborn and no job. Ms. Ruby stepped in. It was a marriage of convenience and shared grief."

"That's a heavy load to carry," LaMarcus says, reaching out to touch her leg. Nia gently moves his hand, knowing that one touch would reignite a fire she's too exhausted to manage.

"I didn't find out the truth until after high school," Nia says, her eyes flashing. "I found letters Claire had written to him that were never mailed. Ms. Ruby kept them. When Dad confronted her, she admitted it. She didn't want him in the picture. She wanted Claire all to herself."

LaMarcus furrows his brow. "She wanted to break them up to keep her friend?"

Nia looks at him, the silence echoing. "LaMarcus... Ms. Ruby is a lesbian. She had an insane, obsessive crush on my mother. She was jealous of my father from the very first second."

"Oh, shit," LaMarcus mutters, rubbing his chin. "That explains... a lot."

"Story time is over," Nia says, her voice snapping back to the present. "We have to get you out of this house."

They perform a tense, silent dance down the stairs. Ms. Ruby is at the dining table, startled as Nia appears. "My word! Don't sneak up on an old woman!" she gasps, clutching her chest.

"Sorry, Ms. Ruby," Nia says, watching LaMarcus hover at the top of the stairs like a ghost.

Ms. Ruby is distracted by a medium-sized brown box. "Maggie Alstead loaned me her catalog to order church hats. I think they're here."

Nia sees her opening. As Ruby fumbles with the tape, Nia waves LaMarcus down. He creeps across the creaky floor, reaching the front door and slipping out. A second later, he opens it from the outside and walks in with a practiced, casual stride.

"Whew! Needed that walk," he says, breathing hard. "How was the market, Ms. Ruby?"

Nia suppresses a sigh of relief as LaMarcus wraps an arm around her, kissing her lips. Ms. Ruby doesn't suspect a thing. She pulls two elaborate hats from the box—one a modest tan, the other a vibrant, fiery red.

"How do I look?" Ruby asks, modeling the red one in the mirror.

"Like Pam Grier in *Foxy Brown*," Nia says, adjusting the brim.

"Red it is," Ruby chirps, glancing at the clock. "12:36. Visitor hours. Let's go see your father."

At the hospital, the news is a godsend. Nurse Sharon informs them that Charlie's tests look great—he's being released tomorrow. The room is filled with laughter as Charlie demands a steak dinner for his homecoming. But Nia can't stop looking at the window. The sun is dipping lower, casting long, skeletal shadows across the parking lot. Kevin's deadline is approaching.

As night falls, they drop a tired Ms. Ruby back at her house. "You two be safe at the market," she calls out, her silhouette framed by the amber glow of the porch light before she disappears inside.

The supermarket is a gauntlet of fluorescent hums and cold air. Nia and LaMarcus move through the aisles like fugitives, their sneakers squeaking against the polished linoleum—a sound that feels loud enough to be a siren. Every time a cart rattles behind them, LaMarcus's shoulders stiffen. They grab the essentials with frantic efficiency, eyes darting toward the automatic doors.

The drive back is quiet, the dashboard lights casting a dim green hue over their faces. Then, the world turns red and blue. The strobe of the police cruiser hits the rearview mirror, blinding and rhythmic. LaMarcus feels his stomach drop into a cold void. He pulls the sedan to the curb, the gravel crunching under the tires like breaking glass.

"Hands on the dash, Nia. Clear as day," LaMarcus whispers, his voice tight, vibrating with a fear he's trying to swallow. A flashlight beam cuts through the side window, jagged and intrusive. A heavy fist thumps the driver's side pillar. The officer, Miller—one of Kevin's inner circles—leans down, his face a mask of bored malice.

"Well, look at this," Miller says, his breath hitching in the cold air. "Out past your bedtime, aren't you, sir?"

"Just coming from the market, Officer," LaMarcus replies. His heart hammers against his ribs, a trapped bird.

"Alright, Step out of the vehicle. Both of you."

The air outside is biting, but the tension is hotter. Miller and his partner, a man with a jagged scar across his chin, don't just search them; they loom. Miller tosses LaMarcus's wallet onto the wet pavement.

"You know, we had a report of shop lifting at the market, tonight. Do know anything g about that?" Miller says, stepping into LaMarcus's personal space. The smell of stale coffee and gunpowder clings to him. He uses a gloved finger to tilt LaMarcus's chin up. "Look at me when you answer my question, boy."

Nia stands shivering against the trunk, the partner's flashlight dancing over her face, purposely blinding her. "We haven't done anything wrong," she says, her voice trembling but defiant.

The partner chuckles, a low, dry sound. "Being in the wrong place at the wrong time is a crime in this neighborhood, sweetheart. Or maybe you're just carrying something you shouldn't be?"

He begins tossing the grocery bags out of the backseat. A carton of eggs shatters on the asphalt; a gallon of milk bursts, the white liquid bleeding into the gutter.

"Hey! That's our food!" Nia cries out, her eyes stinging with frustrated tears.

"Oops," Miller says, grinning without any warmth. He leans in close to LaMarcus's ear, dropping his voice to a predatory silk. "Consider this a courtesy check. Next time, we might not be so polite."

They leave them there in the dark, the cruiser peeling away with a screech of rubber. Nia and LaMarcus stand in the wreckage of their groceries, the silence of the street feeling heavier than the noise that preceded it. The cruiser's taillights fade into two bleeding red dots in the distance, leaving the street in a suffocating, heavy darkness. The smell of burnt rubber and spilled milk hangs in the stagnant air.

LaMarcus doesn't move for a long minute. He stands over the shattered eggs, his hands still trembling, fingers curled into tight, useless fists. Nia is the first to break the trance; she begins grabbing the few salvageable items, her movements jerky and frantic.

"Leave it, Nia," LaMarcus says, his voice sounding hollow, like it's coming from the bottom of a well.

"We paid for this," she snaps back, though the sob catching in her throat betrays her. She drops a bruised apple back into a torn plastic bag and stands up, wiping her damp palms on her jeans.

They climb back into the car. The interior, which felt like a sanctuary ten minutes ago, now feels like a cage. The silence between them is thick with the realization they've both been avoiding. LaMarcus grips the steering wheel at ten and two, his finger tight against the dark leather.

# CHAPTER XII

## Final Showdown

"That wasn't a random stop," Nia says, her voice barely a whisper. She stares out the side window at the rows of darkened houses. "Miller... he's Kevin's cousin's best friend. They grew up on the same block."

LaMarcus finally turns to look at her, his eyes dark with a mix of fury and exhaustion. "I know. He didn't even ask for my registration. He just wanted me to know he could touch us whenever he felt like it."

He slams a palm against the wheel, the sound echoing in the cramped space. "Kevin is using them as his own personal hit squad. He's sitting somewhere right now, laughing because he knows we're sitting here terrified."

Nia reaches over, placing her cold hand over his. "He wants you to react, LaMarcus. He wants you to give them a reason to do more than just break some eggs."

"He's winning, Nia," LaMarcus says, his jaw set so tight it looks like it might snap. "He's got the badge on his side."

The heater kicks on, blowing dry, lukewarm air into the cabin, but it does nothing to cut the chill settling in their bones. LaMarcus puts the car in gear, his eyes scanning the rearview mirror every few seconds, waiting for the red and blue lights to return.

The car rolls to a stop in front of Ms. Ruby's small, weathered frame house. The porch light she left on casts a long, amber rectangle across the overgrown lawn, looking more like a spotlight than a welcome mat.

LaMarcus kills the engine. The sudden silence is deafening, punctuated only by the rhythmic *tick-tick-tick* of the cooling metal under the hood. He stays gripped to the wheel, staring at the front door.

"We can't tell her," Nia says, her voice low and sharp. She's clutching the one grocery bag that didn't split.

LaMarcus turns to her, his brow furrowed in the dim light of the dome lamp. "She's going to ask where the milk is, Nia. She's going to see your coat is damp from the street. She isn't blind."

"If we tell her Kevin is using the police to hunt us, she'll have a heart attack," Nia counters, her eyes pleading. "She already thinks of Kevin like an asshole. This... this would break her heart before it breaks her spirit."

LaMarcus wipes a hand over his face, feeling the grit of the roadside on his skin. "And if we don't tell her? If they show up here? She needs to know the front porch isn't a safe zone anymore."

They step out of the car, the gravel crunching under their boots like a warning. The night air feels thinner now, every shadow under the oak trees looking like a crouched figure. As they climb the porch steps, the floorboards groan under their weight.

The door swings open before they can reach for the handle. Ms. Ruby stands there in her floral robe, a knitted shawl draped over her narrow shoulders. She looks from their empty hands to their pale, haunted faces.

"You're back late," she says, her voice soft but knowing. Her eyes drift to a smudge of road grime on LaMarcus's cheek. "And you look like you've seen a ghost."

LaMarcus opens his mouth to pivot to a lie—something about a flat tire or a closed store—but the words die in his throat when he sees the tremor in Nia's chin.

"It wasn't a ghost, Ms. Ruby," Nia says, her voice trembling as she steps into the warmth of the hallway. "It was Kevin's friends. They... they stopped us."

Ms. Ruby's face doesn't shatter; it hardens. She pulls the shawl tighter around herself, her gaze shifting to the dark street behind them. "The boys in the uniforms?"

LaMarcus nods slowly. "They trashed the groceries. Miller was there."

The old woman stands silent for a moment, the ticking of the hallway clock filling the space. Then, she steps back, gesturing for them to come inside. "Seal the bolt, LaMarcus," she says, her voice regaining its iron. "I'll put the kettle on. If Kevin wants to use the law as a leash, he's forgotten who taught him how to bark. We aren't hiding in the dark tonight."

The cellar door is still ajar when a jagged, metallic screech tears through the quiet of the street. It's the sound of a tire catching a curb. LaMarcus freezes, the brass key biting into his palm. He and Nia exchange a look of pure dread before rushing to the front window. Outside, the world is bathed in the sickly yellow glow of the streetlamp. Kevin's black Metallic Buick is parked crookedly across the sidewalk, one tire resting on Ms. Ruby's manicured grass.

The driver's side door swings open, hanging heavy on its hinges. Kevin stumbles out, his large frame swaying like a tree in a storm. He isn't in his work clothes now; he's in a gray hoodie that's stained at the chest, and his eyes are bloodshot, darting wildly toward the porch. He reeks of expensive bourbon and cheap resentment even from several yards away.

"LaMarcus!" Kevin bellows, his voice thick and slurred, echoing off the quiet houses. "I know you're in there, you bastard! Think you can just hide behind an old woman's skirts?"

He kicks the picket fence, the wood splintering with a pathetic crack. He's laughing, but it's a jagged, ugly sound. He fumbles with his waistband, the heavy silhouette of his off-duty piece visible under his sweatshirt. Nia's breath hitches beside LaMarcus. "He's wasted. LaMarcus, he's going to get someone killed."

Ms. Ruby moves past them both, her gait steady, her face a mask of disappointment. She reaches for the deadbolt.

"Ms. Ruby, don't," LaMarcus warns, reaching for her arm, but she shakes him off with surprising strength.

"Let him see me," she says firmly.

She swings the door open and steps onto the porch, the cold night air rushing into the warm hallway. Kevin stops mid-stride at the bottom of the steps. He blinks, trying to focus on her.

"Aunt Ruby," Kevin sneers, his head lolling to the side. "Tell your houseguest to come out and take his medicine. Miller said he was acting real brave at the market. I want to see that bravery now."

"You look pathetic, Kevin," Ms. Ruby says, her voice carrying across the yard like a whip. "Standing on my lawn, smelling like a gutter, threatening people who have done you no harm. Is this what your mother prayed for?"

Kevin flinches at the mention of his mother, his face twisting into a mask of drunken fury. He takes a lurching step up the first stair. "Don't you bring her into this! This is about respect! Nia thinks she can just slide back into town and showcase her new toy…. embracing me… in my own town! You out yo muthafuckkin mind!"

He points a trembling finger at the door, his eyes landing on Nia as she shadows the doorway. "You think you're safe? I own this zip code! I'm the head nigga in charge!"

LaMarcus steps out onto the porch, shielding Nia, his hand tight around the brass key in his pocket. The metal feels like a loaded gun. "The law is supposed to be sober, Kevin. Go home before you do something you can't undo."

Kevin stares up at him, his hand drifting toward his waistband again, his knuckles twitching. The street is silent, the neighbors' curtains fluttering as they watch the meltdown of the man who is supposed to represent the city in a positive way.

The streetlights flicker, casting long, sickly shadows over the pavement as Nia follows LaMarcus onto the porch. She stays close to his shoulder, her heart drumming against her ribs. The air is thick with the smell of wet asphalt and the sour, heavy stench of bourbon radiating off Kevin.

Down the block, a silver sedan rounds the corner and slows to a crawl. Barbara sits behind the wheel, her face pale in the dashboard light, her eyes wide as she watches the confrontation through her windshield. She doesn't turn off the engine; the low idle is the only sound in the sudden, suffocating silence of the neighborhood.

"You're a disgrace, Kevin," LaMarcus says, his voice low and vibrating with a controlled rage. "Look at you. You can barely stand. This is how you think Nia want to come back to you…a drunk?"

"I don't need to stand to put you in your place," Kevin sneers, his head lolling. He wipes a hand across his mouth, his eyes bloodshot and unfocused. "You come back here, sniffing around what's mine... acting like you're better than me. I'm the one with the power. I'm the one people fear!"

"Nobody fears you, Kevin," Nia interjects, her voice trembling but sharp. "They're just embarrassed for you."

Kevin's face contorts, a mask of pure, drunken malice. "Embarrassed?" he roars. "You think this is a joke?"

He's had enough of the talking. His hand blurs as he reaches into the inner part of his belt, his fingers fumbling with the heavy weight of cold steel. He jerks the weapon free—a massive, silver .44 Magnum that catches the amber glow of the porch light.

"Kevin, no!" Ms. Ruby screams, her voice cracking as she lunges forward.

Kevin ignores her, his arm swaying as he levels the hand cannon directly at Nia's chest. The barrel looks like a dark, bottomless tunnel. His finger tightens on the trigger, his knuckles white.

"Die then!" he barks.

LaMarcus doesn't think. In one explosive motion, he lunges toward Nia, his arm hooking around her waist. "Get down!"

*CRACK.*

# CHAPTER XIII

## When The Dust Settles

The roar of the Magnum is deafening, a physical punch of sound that shatters the night. The muzzle flash illuminates the yard in a blinding strobe of white. Because of the alcohol clouding his vision and the kick of the heavy frame, Kevin's aim wavers at the final microsecond.

LaMarcus throws his weight into Nia, shoving her hard toward the porch boards and falling on top of her. The bullet screams through the air where Nia's head had been a second before. It zips through the fabric of LaMarcus's jacket, hot and biting, grazing the meat of his shoulder with the force of a branding iron.

They hit the wood hard. LaMarcus grunts, a sharp, searing heat blossoming across his shoulder, soaking his shirt in an instant.

"LaMarcus!" Nia gasps, her face pressed against the rough cedar of the porch.

Kevin stands at the bottom of the steps, the gun still smoking in his hand, his eyes wide as the recoil nearly knocks him over. From the street, Barbara slams her car into park, her scream muffled behind the glass of her car.

The roar of the Magnum is still ringing in the air as Nia and LaMarcus hit the porch boards. The heavy .44 slug doesn't just graze LaMarcus; it tears through the meat of his shoulder and continues on, the tumbling lead catching Nia in the upper arm as she falls. They collapse in a heap of tangled limbs and stifled gasps, the scent of copper and burnt gunpowder filling their lungs.

Kevin stands at the base of the steps, the massive revolver trembling in his hand. He looks confused, his drunken mind trying to process the crimson staining LaMarcus's shirt. He raises the gun again, his thumb fumbling to cock the hammer for a second shot.

Suddenly, the screen door doesn't just open—it explodes outward.

Ms. Ruby emerges from the shadows of the hallway, her small frame transformed. She isn't holding a tea service; she's gripped onto a **Mossberg 590 pump**, the packetized steel gleaming under the porch light. Her face is a mask of ancient, righteous fury.

"Not in my house!" she bellows.

*Shuck-sheck.* The sound of the pump action racking a shell is a mechanical death knell.

Before Kevin can even blink, Ms. Ruby unloads. The Mossberg kicks against her shoulder, but she holds her ground like an oak. The blast is a wall of sound that drowns out Kevin's stuttered plea. A cloud of acrid white smoke erupts from the barrel, instantly entangling with the wisps still rising from Kevin's Magnum.

The buckshot catches Kevin square in the chest. The force of the blast lifts him off his feet, his boots skidding on the wet grass as he's slammed backward. He stumbles, his arms flailing, the silver revolver slipping from his numb fingers and vanishing into the tall weeds.

Barbara screams, throwing her car door open and sprinting toward the lawn just as Kevin hits the hood of his SUV with a metallic *thud.*

Nia groans, clutching her arm and rolling to the side of the porch, her breath coming in ragged hitches. Beside her,

LaMarcus rolls onto his back, his hand clamped over his shoulder, blood seeping through his fingers. He looks up, his eyes meeting Ms. Ruby's.

The old woman's chest heaves as she lowers the Mossberg, her eyes darting between the two of them. When she sees them move—sees the life still flickering in their gazes—a sob of pure relief hitches in her throat. "Stay down," she rasps, her voice cracking. "Just stay down."

In the street, Kevin is a ghost of the man who arrived. He staggers blindly toward the driver's side of his car, his hands clutching at his shredded chest. He leans heavily against the hood, his fingers leaving dark, wet streaks on the black paint. His legs give out, and he slides slowly down the side of the vehicle, his back scraping against the metal until he hits the pavement.

He slumps over, his head lolling back against the front tire. His eyes are wide, fixed on the vast, indifferent expanse of the stars above, his breath rattling in his chest as the silence of the night rushes back in.

The copper tang of blood and the acrid sting of gunpowder hang heavy in the night air. From the sidewalk, Barbara freezes. Her boots are planted in the damp grass; her eyes locked on the crumpled figure of Kevin slumped against his tire. This was the man she loved—the man she defended and shielded—now reduced to a broken shadow under the flickering streetlamp.

She doesn't scream. She doesn't run to him. Instead, a hollow, cold terror washes over her face. She stops mid-step, her breath hitching in a jagged sob. Suddenly, she spins on her heel, stumbling back toward her idling sedan. She throws herself into the driver's seat, the engine roaring as she slams it into gear. With a screech of tires that tears through the neighborhood's shocked silence, she pulls a violent U-turn, the headlights sweeping across the grisly scene one last time before she speeds away, fleeing the horror she can no longer fix.

On the porch, the adrenaline begins to ebb into a heavy, throbbing ache. Ms. Ruby exhales a long, shaky breath and sets the **Mossberg 590** down, leaning it carefully against the door frame. Her hands are steady now, fueled by the singular need to protect her own.

"Come on, baby," Ms. Ruby whispers, reaching for Nia. Together, they grip LaMarcus's uninjured side, helping him heave himself upright. LaMarcus hisses through his teeth, his hand clamped over the jagged tear in his shoulder, his eyes never leaving the street.

Below them, Kevin is still fighting. His legs kick feebly against the asphalt, his boots scuffing the ground in a rhythmic, desperate struggle. His arms twitch, reaching for a sky he can no longer see, his chest riddled with the openings left by the buckshot. Each breath is a wet, rattling labor—the sound of a man trying to swallow the night.

Nia detaches herself from LaMarcus's side. She moves down the porch steps, her gait slow and ethereal, like a sleepwalker. She walks across the grass, past the discarded Magnum, until she is standing directly over him.

The struggle stops. Kevin's limbs go limp, the tension draining out of his frame as if a plug had been pulled. A final, thin wheeze of air escapes his lungs—a soft, whistling sigh that signals the end.

Nia looks down at him. For the first time in years, the cruelty has vanished from his features. The sneer is gone; the jagged, predatory edge of his mouth has softened. She watches as peace settles over his face, looking almost like the boy she used to know before the darkness took root. It feels as though a demon has finally been released from its cage, retreating back to some distant, dark cave and leaving only the hollow shell behind.

She stands there in the silence, the wind ruffling her hair, finally breathing air that doesn't feel like it belongs to him.

The night air, once filled with the roar of gunfire, is now overtaken by the rhythmic, pulsing glow of blue and red. It isn't just Miller's crew this time; the street is choked with a fleet of cruisers from a different precinct, their sirens dying into low, mournful chirps.

On the porch, a medic in a neon vest leans over LaMarcus, cutting away the blood-soaked fabric of his shirt. LaMarcus winces as the cool sting of antiseptic meets the raw heat of the graze. Nia sits beside him, her own arm bandaged, her eyes fixed on the driveway.

A seasoned detective—a woman with graying hair and a clipboard—stands at the top of the steps. She looks from the Mossberg 590 leaning against the door frame to the brass key still clutched in LaMarcus's good hand.

"He came here uninvited?" the detective asks, her voice gravelly but neutral.

"He was drunk," Nia says, her voice steady. "He pulled his off-duty piece and fired first. He was going to kill us."

Ms. Ruby stands in the doorway; her hands tucked into the pockets of her robe. She doesn't look like a woman who just fired a shotgun; she looks like a woman who just finished a long day's work. "I protected my home, Detective. I've lived on this block fifty years, and I've never seen anyone act the way that boy did tonight."

Down on the asphalt, the investigators move with clinical efficiency. They bag the silver .44 Magnum found in the grass. They photograph the shattered eggs and the trail of milk that still stains the gutter from earlier that evening. The evidence of Kevin's harassment—the "courtesy check"—is now part of a much larger file.

A pair of EMTs approach the Buick. They don't hurry; there is no pulse to find. With a practiced, heavy silence, they unfurl a crisp white sheet. It flutters for a moment in the breeze before settling over Kevin's face, masking the newfound peace Nia had seen there. As they lift the gurney into the back of the ambulance, the metal wheels clatter against the pavement—the final sound of Kevin leaving the neighborhood.

The detective scribbles a final note and looks at Ms. Ruby. "A neighbor down the street back your story, Ma'am. He fired a .44 into a private residence while intoxicated. You met lethal force with lethal force."

She closes her folder with a definitive snap. "It's a clear case of self-defense. No charges will be filed against you, Ms. Ruby. But I'll need a formal statement down at the station tomorrow."

As the ambulance pulls away without its sirens, the heavy weight that had been crushing the household for months finally begins to lift. The "demon" is gone, and for the first time, the law feels like a shield rather than a weapon.

The next morning, the sun breaks through the clouds with a cruel brilliance. On the way to church, the car rolls over the dark, dried spot in the street where Kevin took his last breath. Ms. Ruby insists on the service, seeking a peace Nia isn't sure she'll ever find in Memphis.

By noon, they drove to the station to give her statement then to the hospital. Charlie is cleared. The drive home is quiet, the radio playing Marvin Gaye.

“Should we tell him about Kevin?” Nia whispers.

“I’ve never kept a secret from that man since those letters,” Ms. Ruby says firmly. “And I won’t start now.”

A couple of day later, the police terminated and arrested officer Miller and his partner for multiple unlawful arrest. The police also were looking for Kevin’s secretary, Barbara, to answer questions about missing ledgers. But she left the city before police can capture her.

"I’ll call you the second we land, Daddy," she whispers, her voice thick.

Charlie offers a weak but steady smile. "Don't you worry about me, baby girl. I’ve got Ms. Ruby to keep me in line. You just go live your life."

Nia nods, blinking back tears, and turns to find Ms. Ruby waiting by the door. The older woman pulls Nia into a hug that smells of cocoa butter and peppermint.

"Take care of my girl, LaMarcus," Ms. Ruby says, reaching out to pat his arm.

"With my life, Ms. Ruby," LaMarcus promises, his voice a low, grounding rumble. "Thank you for everything."

"You all get moving," Ms. Ruby says, shooing them toward the stairs with a wave of her hand, though her eyes remain glassy. "That plane won't wait for sentiment."

The heavy oak front door clicks shut behind them, sounding final. As they climb into the car, the silence of the neighborhood feels breathless. Nia stares out the window as the familiar streets of her youth begin to blur into a haze of grey and green.

"You, okay?" LaMarcus asks softly, his hand finding hers on the center console.

Nia lets out a long, shaky breath, her shoulders finally dropping. "I don't know. It feels like I'm leaving a literal ghost town behind me. I keep waiting to see that grey Buick in the rearview mirror."

LaMarcus squeezes her hand, his thumb tracing circles over her knuckles. "He's gone, Nia. The threat is in the dirt. We're going home."

"Home," Nia repeats, the word tasting like a prayer. "I never thought Detroit would sound like paradise, but I can't wait to see those city lights."

Back in Detroit, the city lights feel like a sanctuary. LaMarcus escorts Nia to her apartment, carrying her bags into the quiet safety of her home.

"Go to bed, baby," he whispers, seeing the hollow exhaustion in her eyes. "I'll be back."

Nia takes a long, hot shower, trying to wash the memory of the Memphis pavement off her skin. While she falls into a deep, dreamless sleep, LaMarcus slips away to his gym. He isn't going to work; he's grabbing a big of his essentials and his folded massage bed. He knows that when she wakes up, she'll need more than just a nap—she'll need to be reminded that she is safe, she is loved, and she is finally free.

# CHAPTER XIV

## Sexual Healing

The two-hour nap acts like a spiritual reset for Nia. She eases the covers off her body, the cool air of the apartment hitting her skin as she stretches toward the ceiling, her spine popping in a satisfying, rhythmic crack. She notices the living room lights are dimmed to a soft, amber glow. *Strange,* she thinks, wondering if she'd bumped the switch on her way in.

She wanders into the hallway, searching for LaMarcus, but the apartment is silent. Just as she turns to head back to her room, a firm, rhythmic knock echoes from the front door. Nia glances at her watch: 7:55 PM.

"Who is it?" she calls out, peering through the peephole.

She sees his tall, broad-shouldered frame posing playfully in the distorted glass. "It's LaMarcus! Here for your eight o'clock appointment!"

Nia throws the deadbolt and swings the door open. He's standing there in a clean grey jogging outfit, a professional-grade massage table and a bag of supplies tucked under his arm.

"LaMarcus, what is all this?" she asks, a tired but curious smile tugging at her lips.

"Good evening, Ma'am," he says, his voice dropping into a smooth, professional baritone. "My name is LaMarcus, and I'm here for your private massage session."

Nia steps aside, a hand over her mouth to hide her amazement. After the trauma of the last past week, the fact that he wants to role-play to ease her mind touches her deeply. She reaches for her phone, clicks the ringer to silent, and sets it face down. She's never done this before—the stranger, the appointment—but she's ready to be someone else for a while.

"I understand you've had an exhausting weekend," LaMarcus says, pushing the sofa aside to make room for his equipment. "And you woke up with some nagging pain in your lower back?"

Nia blinks, momentarily forgetting the script. *Of course, he knows it was exhausting, he was—* she stops herself, catching his blank, professional stare. He's waiting for his client to answer.

"Oh... oh, yes," she says, tracing the V-neck of her shirt with a finger. "I felt a sharp pull when I was stretching. My boyfriend called you right before he had to leave on his... business trip."

LaMarcus suppresses a grin, reaching into his bag and handing her a thick, white cotton robe. "On a business trip? I bet you spend a lot of lonely nights waiting for him."

"You don't know the half of it," Nia retorts, holding the robe with two fingers as if it were a suspicious artifact. "What am I supposed to do with this?"

"If you could undress and slide into that while I set up the ambiance..."

Nia eyes the cheap cotton. "Do you mind if I use my own? I'll be a little more comfortable in silk."

"Your comfort is my priority, Ma'am," he says, his eyes locking onto hers. "I just didn't want to get any oils on your fine garments."

"Your '*stains*' are always welcome on me, baby," Nia blabs, then immediately bites her lip, realizing she broke character. "I mean... you're very courteous, but I prefer my own robe against my skin."

She retreats to the bedroom, catching him watching her exit with a "Grand Canyon" sized grin. She slips out of her clothes, sliding into a sapphire-blue G-string and a matching silk robe. She catches her reflection in the mirror—flushed, expectant—and ties the belt loosely.

When she returns to the living room, the transformation is complete. Two sticks of incense are smoldering, filling the air with the scent of a tropical sunset. Soft jazz hums from a small red radio, and the massage table is draped in plush towels.

"Ready for my close-up, Mr. Spielberg," Nia says, fiddling with the silk knot at her waist.

"This way, Ms. Hollywood," LaMarcus gestures. "Disrobe and lie face-down."

Nia lets the silk fall, revealing the honeyed glow of her skin before stretching out on the padded table. LaMarcus drapes a towel over her lower half, then moves to the wall.

With a single long stride, he reaches the dimmer and lowers the lights until the room is a sanctuary of shadows. He pulls the heavy curtains shut, sealing them in their own private world.

"One hell of an atmosphere you're creating," Nia murmurs into the face cradle.

"I like my clients relaxed," he replies.

The music shifts to Frederick's instrumental of "*Gentle*". Nia hears the *click-pop* of a bottle, then the sound of liquid being warmed between palms. A scent of Cherry Blossom and Mint hits her senses. Then, his hands find her.

He starts at her lower back, just above the line of her G-string. "Mmm... you found that spot," she exhales. His fingers move like a pianist, find-tuning the tension in her muscles. But when he hits the mid-section of her back, Nia flinches. "There—right there. It's shooting down my thigh."

Role-play or not, the stress of Memphis had physically knotted her up. LaMarcus strips off his sweat jacket, revealing a tank top that strained against his chest. "I have an idea, Ms. Jefferson. If you're on board?"

"Whatever you have planned, I'm down," Nia sighs, surrendering completely.

He moves to her feet, cracking each toe with a rhythmic *pop*. He works his way up her calves, his palms firm, pressing the minty heat of the oil into her pores. When he moves the towel to expose her lower back and glutes again, Nia raises her head. "Excuse me, sir? What exactly are you doing?"

"I need room to work the source of your tension, Ma'am," he says with a straight face.

"Well... I suppose you have me there."

For the next couple of minutes, the line between role-play and reality blurs into a haze of sensation. He asks about her "life," and she tells him she's a lead editor, complaining about the "stressful" job. He kneads her muscles with his elbows and fists, his hands working magic she didn't know was possible.

"If you aim to please," Nia whispers, her voice thick with desire, "then start pleasing my ass. I still feel some tension."

LaMarcus chuckles, his hands moving in slow, heavy circles over her hips. Nia reaches back, her fingers trailing up his grey sweatpants until she feels the hard, rhythmic pulse of his manhood through the fabric. He's just as ready as she is. The massage turns into a slow-burn sedation. He slides her G-string off with his teeth, his lips trailing fire down her spine. When he finally flips her over, the air in the room feels electric.

"I hope you don't do this for all your clients," she gasps as his hands find her inner thighs.

"I never mix business with pleasure," he murmurs, hovering over her lips. "Until now..."

The ambience in the living room is thick and heavy, the scent of cherry blossom and mint mingling with the primal heat rising between them. Nia reaches down, her fingers brushing against the soft fabric of his grey jogging pants until they slide past his hips, pooling at his knees. He stands before her, a masterpiece of shadow and muscle in the dim light. His manhood is a testament to the tension of the weekend, a heavy, pulsing weight that hooks slightly, twitching with every frantic beat of his heart. She can see the prominent vein mapping the length of him, a roadmap of the blood and energy ready to be spent.

Nia rises slightly from the table, the cool air of the room hitting her damp skin. She reaches for the small bottle of massage oil on the side table. The *click* of the cap sounds loud in the quiet room. She mimics his earlier gesture, pouring the slick liquid into her palm and rubbing her hands together until they are warm and fragrant. She glides her palm over the length of him, her grip firming with every rhythmic stroke.

"Do you mind if I give you your tip a little early?" Nia whispers, her voice a sultry rasp as she circles the head of his member.

LaMarcus lets out a jagged breath, his head falling back as he bites his bottom lip, his teeth white against his dark skin. "No, Ma'am," he groans, staying deep in the role. "I don’t mind that one bit."

His hands aren't idle. He leans over her, his palms traveling a slow, torturous path from her waist up to her shoulders before settling on her breasts. He kneads the soft weight of her, his thumbs circling her areoles until her nipples are peaked and sensitive.

Then, he ushers his fingers downward. He finds the junction of her inner thighs, his touch light as he coaxes her to open for him. Nia assists him, sliding her heels onto the padded surface of the massage table and spreading her knees wide. His fingers dive into her trim pussy, navigating the slick heat of her until he finds her clitoris.

The rhythm is intoxicating. While her hand maintains a steady, slick friction on his shaft, his digits are working wonders between her legs, slipping inside her and then retreating to massage her center. The pleasure builds until the air in LaMarcus's lungs seems to vanish. He can't take the distance anymore. Without a word, he hooks one of Nia's legs over his broad shoulder and buries his face in her sweet, aching passion.

"OH SHIT!" Nia cries out, her hand flying to her mouth to muffle the sound of her own ecstasy.

She hunches her back off the table, her body arching like a bow as he spreads her labia with his fingers. His tongue is a force of nature—quick, relentless, and focused. It feels like a tornado swirling through a Kansas cornfield, leaving nothing but chaos and heat in its wake. Nia's fingers tangle in the short hair at the back of his head, pinning him to her as he strikes that special spot again and again.

She tries to reach for his groin, wanting to return the favor, but the sensation of his mouth on her is so overwhelming that her arms fall limp at her sides. LaMarcus pauses only for a second to wet his middle and forefingers in his mouth before easing them back into her universe, stretching her and filling her while his tongue continues its frantic work. Nia lets out a long, shuddering sigh of relief, her toes curling tight as she nears the edge of her first real peace in days.

Nia reaches out, her fingers trembling slightly as she taps LaMarcus on the shoulder, a silent command for him to bring his face to hers. He obliges, rising from his knees and meeting her in a deep, soul-shattering kiss that tastes of mint and desperate relief. While their tongues dance, Nia's hand finds him again, her palm traveling down his sweat-slicked stomach to wrap around his throbbing length. She guides him upward, brushing the sensitive tip against her succulent lips, teasing herself with his heat.

Slowly, she swirls her tongue around the crown before taking him inside. LaMarcus groans into the kiss, then pulls back just long enough to shed the rest of his clothes. He kicks his jogging pants aside and yanks the tank top over his head, standing before her in the amber light, fully exposed and magnificent.

Nia opens her mouth wide, her tongue a velvet runway for him to follow. As he slides deep into her throat, a new switch flips inside her; the fear of the weekend is replaced by a primal, driving hunger. She reaches around to his backside, her fingers digging into his firm glutes to pull him even deeper. She gags momentarily as he hits the back of her throat, but she doesn't pull away. Instead, she transitions to her hand, jerking his shaft with a tight, rhythmic grip while she catches her breath, her eyes locked onto his.

"You're doing so good, Ms. Jefferson," LaMarcus rasps, his hands bracing against the edge of the massage table to keep his balance.

Nia smiles around him, her fingernails scraping lightly across his defined six-pack, a sharp contrast to the soft warmth of her mouth as she invites him back in. She plays with the tempo, slowing her movements and gently massaging his weight below to keep him on the edge, refusing to let the moment end too soon.

LaMarcus eventually reaches for her ankle, his grip firm but tender. He waits for her to pull away before sliding her horizontally across the table. He seizes the back of her thighs, spreading her wide, and dives back into her sweetness. He hitches her legs over his shoulders, his tongue exploring every inch of her pleasure zone with a renewed, frantic energy. His hands aren't idle; they glide upward, mapping the curves of her waist and ribs until they reach the "promised land" of her firm, aching breasts.

After several minutes of lost time, LaMarcus rises from his knees. He reaches for a small bottle of lube tucked among the oils on his mini-table. The liquid is cool as he applies it to his pounding manhood, his other hand busy fingering the very heart of her femininity. Nia's head thrashes from left to right on the cushion, her breath coming in short, jagged hitches as she waits for the real thing to replace his digits.

When he finally glides the pulsing head of his manhood over her, the contact is electric. He slides the tip in slowly, savoring the friction.

"Oh, God," Nia exhales, a wave of calmness washing over her even as the passion spikes.

They both let out a long, shaky breath, the anticipation finally giving way to the act. Nia reaches back, her fingers white-knuckled as she grips the end of the table to keep herself from sliding, while LaMarcus thrusts forward, filling her completely. She brings her own hand down, her fingers finding her clitoris to amplify the sparks flying behind her eyelids, riding the rhythm of his body as they finally leave the shadows of Memphis behind.

LaMarcus watches with a surging sense of pride as Nia's breasts bounce in a frantic rhythm with every deep thrust. Her eyes roll back, the whites showing as she loses herself in the sensation, her breath coming in ragged, shallow gasps.

Suddenly, Nia finds a burst of reclaimed energy. She places her palms against his chest and firmly pushes him back. LaMarcus stumbles slightly, his eyes wide with a flash of genuine shock as she slides off the massage table. The cool air hits her damp skin, but she doesn't let the fire cool. She drops to her knees on the plush carpet, taking only the head of his pulsing shaft into her mouth, swirling her tongue with a slow, agonizing tease that makes his knees buckle.

She is relentless. Her hand maintains a steady, slick rhythm on the length of him while her mouth works a different kind of magic. She reaches back, her fingers digging into the firm muscle of his glutes, pulling him in until he is buried deep in her throat. When she finally releases him to catch her breath, she doesn't stop. She uses her free hand to reach between her own thighs, spreading herself open and teasing her own slick heat right before his eyes.

LaMarcus looks down at her, his chest heaving, his gaze locked onto her dark, bedroom eyes. Even now, he refuses to break character. He slides himself back toward her lips, his voice a low, gravelly rumble.

"You like how that feels going down your throat, Ms. Jefferson?"

Nia doesn't say a word; she just nods, her eyes never leaving his. LaMarcus reaches down, his large hands hook under her armpits, and he hauls her up from the floor. He guides her toward the velvet sofa, his touch possessive and urgent.

"Let's see how you handle this position," he commands, his hands steadying her as she bends over the back of the couch.

The living room is a blur of shadows and amber light as he squats behind her. To Nia's surprise, he delivers a sharp, stinging smack to her left cheek—the sound echoing in the quiet room—before pulling her open. He leans in, his tongue tracing a slow, wet path over her most intimate places.

Nia looks back over her shoulder, a breathless, surprised laugh escaping her. "Oh, *really*?"

LaMarcus doesn't answer with words. He rises back to his full height, the head of his shaft grazing against her clitoris as he readies himself. He slides home, the friction of her inner walls tightening around him like a glove. With every rhythmic thrust, the impact sends a ripple through her body, her skin shimmering like waves on a moonlit ocean. He leans forward, his chest pressing against her back, and buries his face in the crook of her neck, his lips trailing hot, desperate kisses over her skin as he claims her all over again.

Nia arches her back, her spine a graceful curve as she reaches behind her, wrapping her arms around LaMarcus's neck. She pulls him closer, anchoring herself to his strength while he moves inside her with a steady, unrelenting rhythm. LaMarcus counters her movement by wrapping one powerful forearm across her breasts and the other around her waist, pinning her against the sofa. Their bodies are a tangled mess of heat and friction, skin slapping against skin in the quiet, dim room.

"Oh shit... I'm about to come!" Nia gasps, the words repeating like a mantra with every deep, sliding thrust.

The weight of his body against hers only intensifies the fire. Every lunge of his pelvis sends a fresh wave of sensation through her, making her feel slick and desperate for more. LaMarcus gently brushes her hair over her shoulder, his mouth finding the sensitive cord of her neck. He sucks at her skin, focused entirely on the tremors beginning to shake her frame. Nia's eyes roll back into her head; she loses her grip on his neck, her fingers digging deep into the sofa cushions as her entire body tightens. She climaxes with a jagged cry, her frustration and fear from the weekend finally melting away into pure, electric release.

Before she can even catch her breath, LaMarcus hauls her up from the sofa. He directs her toward the living room wall with a firm, possessive hand. He positions her like a suspect in a police pat-down—arms high above her head, palms flat against the cool drywall. Directly in front of her face is her framed college degree. In the reflection of the glass, she can see his dark, determined silhouette behind her. He slides back into her, a deep, full entry that makes her knees buckle.

"Don't move," he commands, his voice a low, gravelly vibration against her back.

The passion is so heavy it feels like a physical weight in the air. Nia's fingers claw at the wall, her body climbing upward as if she's trying to escape the very pleasure he's giving her. She spins around in his arms, her mouth crashing into his. They roll into the hallway, a chaotic whirlwind of limbs and heat.

They bounce off the walls with such force that a framed landscape and a small black and white painting of Detroit's Cass Corridor in the 60's clatter to the floor, the glass cracking under the intensity of their movement.

Nia breaks the kiss long enough to kick open the bedroom door. With a sudden burst of strength, she shoves LaMarcus onto the mattress. He bounces back toward the headboard, a surprised but hungry look on his face. Nia pauses to swipe her hair back, her skin glowing and damp with sweat. She sashays toward him, her movements predatory and confident.

She climbs between his legs, taking him into her mouth while her hands roam over the hard ridges of his chest. LaMarcus groans, his back hitting the headboard as his hand find the back of her head, his fingers tangling in her hair.

After a moment, she pulls away, looking up at him with a superior, challenging stare. She climbs higher, straddling his chest until she is hovering over his face. Sweat drips from her chin onto his forehead. Nia lowers herself slowly, squatting over him and pressing her heat against his trim mustache. LaMarcus doesn't hesitate; he cups her plush backside in his large hands, his tongue finding her and tasting the fine, sweet wine of her desire.

The distant, soulful croon of L.T.D.'s "Love Ballad" drifts in from the living room, a smooth contrast to the frantic, wet sounds of their breathing in the bedroom. Nia is lost in the sensation of LaMarcus's tongue; it's a rhythmic, expert intrusion that shatters her last bit of restraint. Her body gives way, her essence escaping in a heavy, pulsing climax that he catches completely. Her legs tremble, struggling to hold her weight as she hovers over him, until he gently slides out from under her.

LaMarcus lies flat against the damp sheets, his eyes dark with a hunger that hasn't faded. He guides her as she repositions herself, his hands steady on her waist. Nia moves slowly, savoring the friction as she eases his heat back inside her.

The slickness of their passion flows down his stiff length as she begins to move. With every descent, his weight smacks against her, a primal rhythm that echoes the beat of the music. LaMarcus lifts one knee, creating a firm backboard for her to lean against, allowing him to penetrate even deeper. His hands stay busy, massaging the small of her back and the flare of her hips, driving her faster. Nia's head falls back, her neck a long line of tension before she breaks again, a second climax rippling through her.

Breathless, Nia rises and looks down at him. He is still fully at attention, a "monster" of a man who seems to have a bottomless reserve of energy. She puts a finger to her lips, biting her nail as she studies him, a playful, predatory smile tugging at her mouth. She isn't finished with him yet.

She swings a leg over his torso and sits tall, leaning forward to claim his mouth in a kiss that tastes of desire. She grinds her hips in a slow circle, cuffing his length between her thighs.

"You aren't going to waste," she whispers against his lips.

She lifts her hips just enough to tease him before plunging back down, her nails digging deep into the hard muscle of his shoulders. She takes every inch of him, her body molding to his in a perfect fit.

"How do you like your tip?" Nia gasps, her pace turning frantic as she feels the rhythmic twitching of his muscles signaling the end of his endurance.

"I'm loving it," LaMarcus groans, his voice a gravelly rumble. His grip on her hips turns iron-clad, his knuckles white. His eyes snap shut, his breath hitching as he reaches the precipice.

Knowing he's at the edge, Nia eases off him. She moves with a dancer's grace, positioning herself at his waist. She takes him into her mouth, her tongue teasing and twisting while her hand roams his chest, pinching his nipple to send one last spike of electricity through his system. When she pulls away, she maintains a firm, rhythmic stroke.

LaMarcus lets out a jagged murmur as he finally releases. Nia's eyes widen—it's like a Fourth of July firework display. The force of it sends his essence arching toward the ceiling before it settles across his stomach and the rumpled sheets.

LaMarcus sinks into the mattress, a look of pure, unadulterated satisfaction crossing his face. He's completed his mission; the trauma of the weekend has been drowned out by the intensity of the night. Nia doesn't pull away. she continues to massage him, watching the pearlescent glaze on her skin. With a slow, sultry look at him, she licks her fingers clean, savoring the taste of their victory.

They collapse into each other's arms, their skin tacky and warm as they tangle together under the comforter. Outside the window, the moon reaches its peak, hanging like a silver coin over a quiet Detroit, as midnight drifts into the early hours of Monday morning.

# CHAPTER XV

## Walk On By

When the sun finally creeps through the blinds at 6:00 AM, the radio alarm plays "Hello Detroit" by Sammy Davis Jr... Nia feels every muscle in her body—tender, but finally at peace. She makes herbal tea, watching the city wake up, when LaMarcus wraps his arms around her from behind.

"Good morning, beautiful," he whispers.

"Morning, darling. Omelets?"

"No time," he sighs, leaning his forehead against hers. "I've got fires to put out at the gym. Troy's been... distracted. Got a text from him having personal issues with his ex. I think she's leaching him dry or something, but I need to take his client at this morning."

Nia sips her tea, a thought forming. "That reminds me. Janet was asking if you had any... available friends. I mentioned Troy to her, but I didn't know his background like that."

LaMarcus pulls back, eyebrows raised. "Janet? ….. 6'1" Janet…. Janet Waters? You're playing matchmaker now?"

"She wants a 'LaMarcus' of her own," Nia says, letting her robe slip just enough to be a distraction. "Can you see if he wants to go out with her? "

"I'll check with him," LaMarcus says, his voice dropping a heavy octave as his gaze lingers on her. He leans in, his shadow stretching across the kitchen tile as he cages her against the counter. The morning light catches the gold in his eyes, turning his look into something hungry and deliberate.

He pauses, just inches from her face, his thumb tracing the line of her jaw. "But before I go..." he murmurs, his breath warm against her skin, "I think I need a sample of that 'stress-free' session to start my day off right."

Nia's heart skips, her fingers tightening around her tea mug. "LaMarcus, you've got fires to put out," she whispers, though she's already leaning into him.

"The gym can wait ten more minutes," he replies. He captures her lips in a slow, deep kiss that tastes like the herbal mint of her tea and the lingering heat of the night before. His hands slide under the silk of her robe, finding the small of her back and pulling her flush against him, effectively erasing any thoughts of the outside world.

Later that morning, Nia is back in her routine, jogging through the crisp Detroit air. She takes a detour to a small repair shop, pulling a dusty business card from her pocket. *Mr. Jenkins.* She remembers the kind man from the bus station a year ago who told her to stop by if she ever needed help.

She walks into the shop, surrounded by old TVs and humming appliances. A young woman, Sophia, greets her.

"I'm looking for Mr. Jenkins," Nia says with a warm smile. "He gave me his card a while back. Just wanted to say hello."

The light leaves Sophia's eyes. She looks down at the counter, her shoulders sagging. "I'm sorry to tell you this, Ma'am... but my father passed away six months ago. Heart attack."

Nia's smile vanishes, replaced by a cold knot in her stomach. The man who had offered her a literal lifeline when she was running for her life was gone.

Nia gasps, her hand flying to her chest as the air leaves her lungs. The news hits her like a physical blow, vibrating through the small shop filled with the scent of ozone and old solder. Though their encounter at the bus station a year ago was brief, Mr. Jenkins had been the first person to offer her a glimpse of safety when she was running for her life.

"I'm so sorry, Sophia," Nia says, her voice thick with genuine grief as she walks toward the register. "Your father was a great man. He helped me at my lowest point—he gave me hope when I had absolutely nothing."

Sophia's eyes shimmer with unshed tears, and for the next hour, the shop becomes a sanctuary. They talk about their lives, their losses, and the strange way people enter our lives exactly when we need them. Nia leaves with a promise to return, her heart heavy with the guilt of not visiting sooner, but her soul feels tethered to something real.

The morning sun is high now, baking the Detroit pavement as Nia finishes her route. She reaches her favorite spot on Belle Isle. The air is crisp after the overnight storms, smelling of wet earth and river water. The island is alive; geese waddle out of the shimmering pond, pecking rhythmically at the lush grass for breakfast.

Nia sinks onto her usual bench, her body humming from the run. She watches the sunlight dance on the water, soaking in the Vitamin D she desperately needs. Her biggest worries are finally buried—literally—under a slab of concrete back at Memphis Memorial.

A car backfires in the distance, a sharp *crack* that echoes across the park. Nia flinches, her heart racing for a split second as the memory of Kevin's final moment flashes behind her eyes. But as the smoke of the memory clears, she forces a deep breath. The healing has begun. She is ready to love herself, to spread that love, and to leave the ghosts in the South.

She rises from the bench, ready to head home, when she slams right into a tall woman who seems to have appeared out of thin air.

"Oh! Excuse me!" Nia says, catching her balance. "I'm so sorry, I've got a lot on my mind this morning."

The woman is dressed in a light summer dress paired with a thin windbreaker. Large, dark-tinted glasses mask her eyes, and she clutches a grease-stained doughnut shop bag in her right hand.

"Understand," the woman replies, her voice smooth and carefully neutral. "I hope you have a blessed day."

Nia pauses, her head tilting to the side. There is something in the set of the woman's jaw, a familiar sharpness to her facial structure that tugs at a locked door in Nia's memory. "Wait... haven't we met before?"

The stranger offers a thin, practiced smile. "No. I get that question often. I must just have one of those familiar faces."

Nia shrugs, offering a polite smile in return. "Must be. Have a wonderful day."

Nia by side the woman and begins a light jog toward the bridge, her ponytail swinging behind her. She doesn't look back. If she had, she would have seen the woman slide those tinted glasses down the bridge of her nose, revealing eyes that are cold, calculating, and fixed firmly on Nia's back.

It is Barbara, Kevin's side piece who watched him die through her eyes. She sits on Nia's favorite bench, the wood still warm from Nia's body. She pulls a poppy seed bagel from the bag, the scent of yeast and salt filling the air. Her arrival in the Motor City is a calculated cocktail of pleasure and cold-blooded revenge. To Barbara, "sorry" doesn't cover the fact that Kevin is no longer breathing.

She takes a slow, deliberate bite of her breakfast, crossing one leg over the other. Her foot shakes with a restless, manic energy. She watches the geese, her mind already spinning the web of her plan. She won't rest until Nia Jefferson pays for the grave she left behind in Memphis.

www.ingramcontent.com/pod-product-compliance
Lightning Source LLC
LaVergne TN
LVHW090611110826
845146LV00001B/337

* 9 7 9 8 9 9 5 4 6 3 7 0 2 *